"Don't you ever walk out on me like that again!" he bit out.

"I'm a free agent and I can do exactly as I please!"

"You think so?" His mouth hardened with lust. "Well, in that case, so can I!"

Without warning, he pulled her right up against him—so close that she could feel every hard sinew of his body, which seemed to contrast against the softness of her own. A body that should have wanted to resist him, just as she was resisting his demand that she marry him. But it seemed that her body had other ideas. To her horror, she found herself wanting to sink against him. Into him.

Did he sense that? Was that why he gathered her closer still with a small moan of what sounded like his own surrender?

In the pale light, he tilted her face up. "Now, this *is* a time when the word *want* is appropriate. And you want me, Laura, just as I want you. Don't ask me why, but I do," he ground out as he drove his mouth down onto hers.

Dear Reader,

Harlequin Presents® is all about passion, power and seduction—along with oodles of wealth and abundant glamour. This is the series of the rich and the superrich. Private jets, luxury cars and international settings that range from the wildly exotic to the bright lights of the big city! We want to whisk you away to the far corners of the globe and allow you to escape to and indulge in a unique world of unforgettable men and passionate romances. There is only one Harlequin Presents. And we promise you the world....

As if this weren't enough, there's more! More of what you love every month. Two weeks after the Presents titles hit the shelves, four Presents EXTRA titles join them! Presents EXTRA is selected especially for you—your favorite authors and much-loved themes have been handpicked to create exclusive collections for your reading pleasure. Now there are more excuses to indulge! Each month, there's a new collection to treasure—you won't want to miss out.

Harlequin Presents—still the original and the best!

Best wishes,

The Editors

Sharon Kendrick

CONSTANTINE'S
DEFIANT MISTRESS

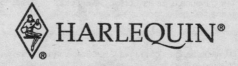

HARLEQUIN®

TORONTO • NEW YORK • LONDON
AMSTERDAM • PARIS • SYDNEY • HAMBURG
STOCKHOLM • ATHENS • TOKYO • MILAN • MADRID
PRAGUE • WARSAW • BUDAPEST • AUCKLAND

Recycling programs
for this product may
not exist in your area.

ISBN-13: 978-0-373-12862-4

CONSTANTINE'S DEFIANT MISTRESS

First North American Publication 2009.

Copyright © 2009 by Sharon Kendrick.

All about the author...
Sharon Kendrick

When I was told off as a child for making up stories, little did I know that one day I'd earn my living by writing them!

To the horror of my parents, I left school at sixteen and did a bewildering variety of jobs: I was a London DJ (in the now-trendy Primrose Hill!), a decorator and a singer. After that I became a cook, a photographer and eventually a nurse. I waitressed in the south of France and drove an ambulance in Australia. I saw lots of beautiful sights, but could never settle down. Everywhere I went I felt like a square peg—until one day I started writing again, and then everything just fell into place. I felt the way Cinderella must have done when the glass slipper fit!

Today I have the best job in the world—writing passionate romances for Harlequin® Books. I like writing stories that are sexy and fast-paced, yet packed full of emotion—stories that readers will identify with, that will make them laugh and cry.

My interests are many and varied—chocolate and music, fresh flowers and bubble baths, films and cooking, and trying to keep my home from looking as if someone's burgled it! Simple pleasures—you can't beat them!

I live in Winchester (one of the most stunning cities in the world, but don't take my word for it—come see for yourself!) and regularly visit London and Paris. Oh, and I love hearing from my readers all over the world...so I think it's over to you!

With warmest wishes,

Sharon Kendrick
www.SharonKendrick.com

CHAPTER ONE

IT WAS hearing his name on the radio which made her senses scream. Laura never had time for newspapers—even if her dyslexia hadn't made reading so difficult—she relied on the morning news programme to keep her up to date. Usually she only listened with half an ear, and usually she wasn't remotely interested in anything to do with international *finance.*

But Karantinos was an unusual name. And it was Greek. And didn't anything to do with that beautiful and ancient land put her senses on painful alert for very obvious reasons?

She had been busy making bread—sprinkling a handful of seeds into the dough before she popped the last batch into the oven. But with shaking hands she stopped dead-still and listened—like a small animal who had found itself caught alone and frightened in the middle of a hostile terrain.

'Greek billionaire Constantine Karantinos has announced record profits for his family shipping line,' intoned the dry voice of the news-reader. 'Playboy Karantinos is currently in London to host a party at the Granchester Hotel, where it is rumoured he will announce his engagement to Swedish supermodel Ingrid Johansson.'

Laura swayed, gripping the work surface to support

herself, her ears scarcely able to bear what she had just heard, her heart pounding with a surprisingly forceful pain. Because she had preserved Constantine in her heart, remembering him just as he'd been when she'd known him—as if time had stood still. A bittersweet memory of a man who still made her ache when she thought of him. But time never stood still—she knew that more than anyone.

And what had she expected? That a man like Constantine would stay single for ever? As if that lazy charm and piercing intellect—that powerhouse body and face of a fallen angel—would remain unattached. She was just surprised that it hadn't happened sooner.

She could hear the sounds of movement from above as she took off her apron. But her heart was racing as she mechanically went through her morning routine of tidying up the kitchen before going upstairs to wake her son. She often told herself how lucky she was to live 'over the shop', and although helping run a small baker's store hadn't been her life's ambition, at least it gave her a modest income which she supplemented with occasional waitressing work. But most of all it provided a roof over their heads—which was security for Alex—and that was worth more than anything in Laura's eyes.

Her sister Sarah was already up, yawning as she emerged from one of the three poky bedrooms, running her fingers through the thick dark curtain of her hair, which so contrasted with her sister's finer, fairer mane.

'Mornin', Laura,' Sarah mumbled, and then blinked as she saw her older sister's face 'What the hell's happened? Don't tell me the oven's gone on the blink again?'

Mutely, Laura shook her head, then jerked it in the direction of her son's bedroom. 'Is he up yet?' she mouthed.

Sarah shook her head. 'Not yet.'

Laura glanced at the clock on the wall, which dominated her busy life, and saw that she had ten minutes before she had to get Alex up for school. Pulling Sarah into the small sitting room which overlooked the high street, she shut the door behind them and turned to her sister, her whole body trembling.

'Constantine Karantinos is in London,' she began, the whispered words falling out of her mouth like jagged little fragments of glass.

Her sister scowled. 'And?'

Laura willed her hands to stop shaking. 'He's throwing a party.' She swallowed. 'And they say he's getting engaged. To a Swedish supermodel.'

Sarah shrugged. 'What do you want me to say? That it's a surprise?'

'No… But I…'

'But what, Laura?' demanded Sarah impatiently. 'You can't seem to accept that the no-good bastard you slept with hasn't an ounce of conscience. That he *never gave you another thought.*'

'He—'

'He what? Refused to see you? Why, you couldn't even get a single meeting with the great man, could you, Laura? No matter how many times you tried. He's never even taken your phone calls! You were good enough to share his bed—but not good enough to be recognised as the mother of his child!'

Laura shot an agonised look at the closed door, straining her ears as she wondered if Alex had done the unheard-of and managed to get himself out of bed without his mother or his auntie gently shaking him awake. But then, seven-year-old boys were notoriously bad at getting up in the morning, weren't they? And they became increasingly curious as they got older…kept asking questions she wasn't sure how to answer…

'Shh. I don't want Alex to hear!'

'Why not? Why shouldn't he know that his father happens to be one of the richest men on the planet—while his mother is working her fingers to the bone in a bread shop, trying to support him?'

'I don't want to…' But her words tailed off. Didn't want to *what* exactly? Laura wondered. Didn't want to hurt her beloved son because it was the duty of every mother to protect her child? Yet she had been finding it increasingly difficult to do that. Just last month Alex had come home with a nasty-looking bruise on his cheek, and when she had asked him what had happened he had mumbled and become very defensive. It had only been later that she'd discovered he'd been involved in some kind of minor skirmish in the playground. And later still that she had discovered the cause, when she'd gone tearing into the school, white-faced and trembling, to seek a meeting with the headmistress.

It transpired that Alex was being bullied because he looked 'different'. Because his olive skin, black eyes and towering height made him look older and tougher than the other boys in his class. And because the little girls in the class—even at the tender ages of six and seven—had been following the dark-eyed Alex around like eager little puppies. Like father, like son, she had thought with a pang.

Laura had felt a mixture of troubled emotions as she'd gone home that day. She'd wanted to ask her son why he hadn't hit back—but that would have gone against every-thing she had taught him. She had brought him up to be gentle. To reason rather than to lash out. For two pins she would have withdrawn her son from the school and sent him somewhere else—but she didn't have the luxury of choice. The next nearest state school was in the neighbouring town, and not only did Laura not have a car but the bus service was extremely unreliable.

Lately her son had been asking her more and more frequently about *why* he looked different. He was an intelligent little boy, and sooner or later he wouldn't allowed her to fob him off with vague and woolly pieces of information about a father he had never seen. If only Constantine would just *talk* to her. Acknowledge his son. Spend a little time with him—that was all she wanted. For her beloved boy to know a little of his heritage.

She was distracted while she gave Alex his breakfast, and even more distracted during the short walk to his school. Although it was almost the summer holidays, the weather had been awful lately—nothing but rain, rain, rain—and this morning the persistent drizzle seemed to penetrate every inch of her body. She shivered a little, and tried to chatter brightly, but she felt as if she had a heavy lead weight sitting in the pit of her stomach.

Alex looked up at her with his dark olive eyes and frowned. 'Is something wrong, Mum?' he questioned.

Your father is about to marry another woman and will probably have a family with her. Telling herself that the blistering shaft of jealous pain was unreasonable under the circumstances, she hugged her son to her fiercely as she said goodbye.

'Wrong? No, nothing's wrong, darling.' She smiled brightly, and watched as he ran into the playground, praying that the head teacher's recent lecture on bullying might have had some effect on the little savages who had picked on him.

She was lost in thought as she walked back to the shop. Hanging up her damp coat in the little cloakroom at the back, she grimaced at the pale face which stared back at her from the tiny mirror hung on the back of the door. Her grey eyes looked troubled, and her baby-fine hair clung to her head like a particularly unattractive-looking skull-cap. Carefully, she brushed it and shook it, then crumpled it into a damp pleat on top of her head.

Pulling on her overall, she was still preoccupied as she walked into the shop, where her sister was just putting on the lights. Five minutes until they opened and the first rush of the day would begin—with villagers keen to buy their freshly baked bread and buns. Laura knew how lucky she was to have the life she had—lucky that her sister loved Alex as much as she did.

The two girls had been orphaned when Sarah was still at school, after their widowed mother had died suddenly and quietly in the middle of the night. A stricken Laura had put her own plans of travelling the world on hold, unsure what path to take to ensure that Sarah could continue with her studies. But fate had stepped in with cruel and ironic timing, because Laura had discovered soon after that she was carrying Alex.

Money had been tight, but they had been left with the scruffy little baker's shop and the flat upstairs, where they had spent most of their childhood years. They had always helped their mother in the shop, so Laura had suggested modernising it and carrying on with the modest little family business, and Sarah had insisted on studying part-time so that she could help with Alex.

Up until now the scheme had worked perfectly well. And if the shop wasn't exactly making a huge profit, at least they were keeping their heads above water and enjoying village life.

But recently Sarah had started talking longingly of going to art school in London, and Laura was horribly aware that she was holding her back. She couldn't keep using her little sister as a part-time child-minder, no matter how much Sarah loved her nephew—she needed to get out there and live her own life. But then how on earth would Laura cope with running a business and being as much of a hands-on mum as she could to Alex? To Alex who was becoming increasingly curious about his background.

Sarah was giving the counter a final wipe, and looked up as Laura walked into the shop. 'You still look fed up,' she observed.

Laura stared down at the ragged pile of rock-cakes and boxes of home-made fudge under the glass counter. 'Not fed up,' she said slowly. 'Just realising that I can't go on hiding my head in the sand any longer.'

Sarah blinked. 'What are you talking about?'

Laura swallowed. Say it, she thought. Go on—*say* it. Speak the words out loud—that way it will become real and you'll *have* to do it. Stop being fobbed off by the gate-keepers who surround the father of your son. Get out there and *fight* for Alex. 'Just that I've got to get to Constantine and tell him he has a son.'

Sarah's eyes narrowed. 'Why the new fervour, Laura?' she asked drily. 'Is it because Constantine is finally settling down? You think that he's going to take one look at you and decide to dump the Swedish supermodel and run off into the sunset with you?'

Laura flushed, knowing that Sarah spoke with the kind of harsh candour which only a sister could get away with—but her words were true. She had to rid herself of any romantic notions where the Greek billionaire was concerned. As if Constantine would even *look* at her now! He certainly wouldn't fancy her any more—for hadn't hard work and a lack of time to devote to herself meant that her youthful bloom had faded faster than most? At twenty-six she sometimes felt—and looked—a whole decade older than her years. And even if the fire in her heart still burned fiercely for the father of her son she had to douse the flames completely.

'Of course I don't,' she said bitterly. 'But I owe it to Alex. Constantine has *got* to know that he has a son.'

'I agree. But aren't you forgetting something?' questioned Sarah patiently. 'Last time you tried to contact him you got precisely nowhere—so what's changed now?'

What *had* changed? Laura walked slowly towards the door of the shop. She wasn't sure—only that perhaps she'd realised time was running out, that maybe this was her last chance. And that she was no longer prepared to humbly accept being knocked back by the tight circle which surrounded the formidable Greek. She was fired up by something so powerful that it felt as if it had invaded her soul. She was a mother, and she owed it to her son.

'What's changed?' Slowly, Laura repeated Sarah's words back to her. 'I guess *I* have. And this time I'm going to get to him. I'm going to look him in the eye and tell him about his son.'

'Oh, Laura, exactly the same thing will happen!' exclaimed Sarah. 'You'll be knocked back and won't get within a mile of him!'

There was a pause. Laura could hear the ticking of her wristwatch echoing the beating of her heart. 'Only if I go the conventional route,' she said slowly.

Sarah's eyes narrowed. 'What are you talking about?'

Laura hadn't really known herself up until then, but it was one of those defining moments where the answer seemed so blindingly simple that she couldn't believe she hadn't thought of it before. Like when she'd decided that they ought to start making their own loaves on the premises rather than having them delivered from the large bakery in the nearby town—thereby enticing their customers in with the delicious smell of baking bread.

'The radio said he's giving some big party in London,' she said, piecing her whirling thoughts into some kind of order. 'In a hotel.'

'And?'

Laura swallowed. 'And what industry has the fastest turn-over of staff in the world? The catering industry! Think about it, Sarah. They'll…they'll need loads of extra staff for the night, won't they? Casual staff.'

'Just a minute…' Sarah's eyes widened. 'Don't tell me you're planning—'

Laura nodded, her heart beating faster now. 'I've done waitressing jobs at the local hotel for years. I can easily get a reference.'

'Okay, so what if you do manage to get on the payroll?' Sarah demanded. 'Then what? You're going to march over to Constantine in your uniform, in the middle of his fancy party, and announce to him in front of the world, not to mention his soon-to-be wife that he has a seven-year-old son?'

Laura shook her head, trying not to feel daunted by the audacity of her own idea but her fervour refused to be dampened. 'I'll try to be a bit more subtle about it than that,' she said. 'But I'm not going to leave until he's in full possession of the facts.'

She reached up and turned over the sign on the shop door from 'Closed' to 'Open'. Already there was a small cluster of shoppers waiting, shaking off the raindrops from their umbrellas as they filed into the shop.

Laura pinned a bright smile to her lips as she stood behind the counter and took her first order, but the irony of her plan didn't escape her. After all, she had been waitressing when she'd first met Constantine Karantinos, and had tumbled into his arms with embarrassing ease.

Afterwards she had looked back and wondered how she could have behaved in a way which had been so completely out of character. And yet it had been such a golden summer in those carefree months before her mother had died, and she'd felt as if she had the world at her feet as she saved up to go travelling.

She had been an innocent in every sense of the word—but a few months of waitressing in a busy little harbour town had trained her well in how to deal with the well-heeled customers who regularly sailed in on their yachts.

Constantine had been one of them, and yet unlike any of them—for he'd seemed to break all the rules. He'd towered over all the other men like a colossus—making everyone else fade into insignificance. The day she had first set eyes on him would be imprinted on her mind for ever; he had looked like a Greek god—his powerful body silhouetted against the dying sun, his dark and golden beauty suggesting both vigour and danger.

She remembered how broad his shoulders had been, and how silky the olive skin which had sheathed the powerful muscle beneath. And she remembered his eyes, too—as black as ebony yet glittering like the early-morning sunlight on the sea. How could she have resisted a man who had seemed like all her youthful fantasies come to life—a man who had made her feel like a woman for the first and only time in her life?

She remembered waking up in his arms the next morning to find him watching her, and she had gazed up at him, searching his face eagerly for some little clue about how he might feel. About her. About them. About the future.

But in the depths of those eyes there had been...nothing.

Laura swallowed.

Nothing at all.

CHAPTER TWO

'YES, Vlassis,' Constantine bit out impatiently, as he glanced up at one of his aides, who was hovering around the door in the manner he usually adopted when he was about to impart news which his boss would not like. 'What is it?'

'It's about the party, *kyrios*,' said Vlassis.

Constantine's mouth flattened. Why had he ever agreed to have this wretched party in the first place? he found himself wondering. Though in his heart he knew damned well. Because there had been too many mutterings for much too long about people in London wanting to enjoy some of the legendary Karantinos wealth. People always wanted to get close to him, and they thought that this might give them the opportunity. And it was always interesting to see your friends and your enemies in the same room—united by those twin emotions of love and hate, whose boundaries were so often blurred.

'What about it?' he snapped. 'And please don't bother me with trivia, Vlassis—that's what I pay other people to deal with.'

Vlassis looked pained, as if the very suggestion that he

should burden his illustrious employer with trivia was highly offensive to him. 'I realise that, *kyrios*. But I've just received a message from Miss Johansson.'

At the mention of Ingrid, Constantine leaned back in his chair and clasped his fingers together in reflective pose. He knew what the press were saying. What they always said if he was pictured with a woman more than once. That he was on the verge of marrying, as most of his contemporaries had now done. His mouth flattened again.

Perhaps one of the greatest arguments in favour of marriage would be having a wife who could deal with the tiresome social side of his life. Who could fend off the ambitious hostesses and screen his invitations, leaving him to get on with running the family business.

'And?' he questioned. 'What did Miss Johansson say?'

'She asked me to tell you that she won't be arriving until late.'

'Did she say why?'

'Something about her photo-shoot overrunning.'

'Oh, did she?' said Constantine softly, his black eyes narrowing in an expression instinctively which made Vlassis look wary.

Unlocking his fingers, Constantine raised his powerful arms above his head and stretched, the rolled-up sleeves of his silk shirt sliding a little further up over the bunched muscle. Slowly he brought his hands down again, lying them flat on the surface of the large desk. The faint drumming of two fingers on the smooth surface was the only outward sign that he was irritated.

Ingrid's coolness was one of the very qualities which had first attracted him to her—that and her white-blonde Swedish beauty, of course. She had a degree in politics, spoke five languages with effortless fluency—and, standing at just over six feet in her stockinged feet, she was one of the few women he had ever met who was able to look him in the eye. Constantine's mouth curved into an odd kind of smile. As well as being one of the few *natural* blondes he'd known…

When they'd met, her unwillingness to be pinned down, her elusiveness when it came to arranging dates, had contrived to intrigue him—probably because it had never happened before. Most women pursued him with the ardour of a hunter with prized quarry in their sights.

But over the months Constantine had realised that Ingrid's evasiveness was part of a game—a master-plan. Beautiful enough to be pursued by legions of men herself, she had recognised the long-term benefits of playing hard-to-get with a man like him. She must have realised that Constantine never had to try very hard, so she had made him try very hard indeed. And for a while it had worked. She had sparked his interest—rare in a man whose natural attributes and huge wealth meant that his appetite had become jaded at an early age.

She had been playing the long game, and Constantine had allowed himself to join in; Ingrid knew what she wanted—to marry an exceptionally wealthy man—and deep down he knew it was high time he took himself a wife. And surely the best kind of wife for a man like him was one who made few emotional demands?

He didn't want some clingy, needy female who thought that the world revolved around him. No, Ingrid came close to fitting almost all his exacting criteria. Every hoop he had presented her with she had jumped through with flying colours. Why, even his father approved of her. And, although the two men had never been close, Constantine had found himself listening for once.

'Why the hell don't you marry her?' he had croaked at his son, where once—before age and ill-health—he would have roared. 'And provide me with a grandson?'

Good question—if you discounted his father's own foolish views on love. Didn't there come a time when every man needed to settle down and produce a family of his own? A boy to inherit the Karantinos fortune? Constantine frowned. Circumstances seemed to have been urging him on like a rudderless boat—and yet something about the sensible option of marrying Ingrid had made him hold back, and he couldn't quite work out what it was.

How long since they had seen one another? Constantine allowed his mind to flick back over the fraught and hectic recent weeks, largely filled with his most recent business acquisition. It had been ages since Ingrid had been in his bed, he realised. Their paths had been criss-crossing over the Atlantic while their careers continued their upward trajectory. Constantine gave a hard smile.

'What time is she arriving?' he questioned.

'She hopes before midnight,' said Vlassis.

'Let's hope so,' commented Constantine, as a faint feeling of irritation stirred within him once more. But he turned to a pile of papers—to the delicate complexity of an offshore deal he was handling. And, as usual, work provided a refuge from the far more messy matter of relationships. For Constantine had learned his lesson earlier than most—that they brought with them nothing but pain and complications.

He left the office around six and headed for the Granchester, whose largest penthouse suite he always rented whenever he was in town. He loved its glorious setting, overlooking lush green parkland, its quiet luxury and the discretion of its staff. And he liked London—just as he liked New York—even if they were too far from the sea for him to ever let complete relaxation steal over him....

To the sound of opera playing loudly on the sound system, he took a long, cold shower before dressing in the rather formal attire which the black-tie dinner warranted. His eyes glittered back at him as he cast a cursory glance at himself in the mirror.

Slipping on a pair of heavy gold cufflinks, he made his way downstairs, his eyes automatically flicking over to his people, who were discreetly peppering the foyer. He knew that his head of security would be unable to prevent the paparazzi from milling around by the entrance outside, but there was no way any of them would be getting into the building to gawp at the rich and the powerful.

Ignoring the gazes of the women who followed his progress with hungry eyes, he walked into the ballroom and looked around. The Granchester had always been a byword for luxury—but tonight the hotel had really surpassed itself. The ballroom was filled with scented blooms, and chandeliers dripped their diamond lights...

A soft voice cut into his thoughts.

'Could...could I get you a drink, sir?'

For a brief moment the voice stirred a distant memory—as faint as a breath on a still summer's day. But then it was gone, and slowly Constantine turned to find a waitress standing staring up at him—chewing at her lip as if she hadn't had eaten a meal in quite a while. His eyes flicked over her. With her small, pinched face and tiny frame she looked as if she probably *hadn't* eaten a meal in ages.

Something in her body language made him pause. Something untoward. He frowned.

'Yes. Get me a glass of water, would you?'

'Certainly, sir.' Miraculously, Laura kept her voice steady, even though inside she felt the deep, shafting pain of rejection at the way those black eyes had flicked over her so dismissively. She had tried to hold his look for as long as was decently possible under the circumstances—willing him to look at her with a slowly dawning look of incredulity. But instead, what logic told her would happen *had* happened. *The father of her son hadn't even recognised her!*

Yet had she really bought into the fantasy that he might? That he would stare into her eyes and tell her that they looked like the storm clouds which gathered over his Greek island? He had said that when he had been charming her into his bed, and doubtless he would have something suitable in his repertoire for any woman. Something to make every single woman feel special, unique and amazing. Something which would make a woman willingly want to give him her virginity as if it were of no consequence at all.

It had been her moment to tell him that he had a beautiful little son—while there was no sign of the supermodel girlfriend all the papers had been going on about—and she had blown it. The shock of seeing him again, coupled with the pain of realising that she didn't even qualify as a memory, had made her fail to seize the opportunity. But surely you couldn't just walk up to a man who was essentially a total stranger and come out with a bombshell like that?

Laura hid her trembling fingers in her white apron as she quickly turned away—but the emotional impact of seeing Constantine again made her stomach churn and her heart thump so hard that for a moment she really thought she might be sick.

But she couldn't afford to be sick. She had to stay alert—to choose a moment to tell him what for him would be momentous news. And it wasn't going to be easy. Getting an agency placement to waitress at the Karantinos party had been the easy bit—the hard stuff was yet to come.

'What the hell do you think you're doing?' demanded a severely dressed middle-aged woman as Laura walked up to the bar to place her order.

Laura smiled nervously at the catering manager, who had summoned all the agency staff into a cramped and stuffy little room half an hour earlier to tell them about the high expectations of service which every Granchester customer had a right to expect. 'I just offered the gentleman a drink—'

'Gentleman? *Gentleman*? Do you know who that *is*?' the woman hissed. 'He's the man who's *giving* this party which is paying your wages! He's a bloody world-famous Greek shipping tycoon—and if anyone is going to be offering him drinks then it's going to be me. Do you understand? I'll take over from now on. What did he ask for?'

'Just…just water.'

'Still or sparkling?'

'He…he didn't say.'

The manager's eyes bored into her. 'You mean you didn't ask?'

'I…I… No, I'm sorry, I'm afraid I didn't.' Inwardly, Laura squirmed beneath the look of rage on her supervisor's face, and as the woman opened her mouth to speak she suspected that she was about to be fired on the spot. But at that moment there was some sort of hubbub from the other end of the ballroom, as the harpist arrived and began making noisy demands, and the manager gave Laura one last glare.

'Just do what you're supposed to do. Offer him both still and sparkling, and then fade into the background—you shouldn't find *that* too difficult!' she snapped, before hurrying away towards the musician.

Laura tried to ignore the woman's waspish words as she carried her tray towards Constantine. But inside she was trembling—mainly with disbelief that she had managed to get so close to him. And thrown into the complex mix of her emotions at seeing him again was also her body's unmistakable reaction to seeing the biological father of her son. It was something she stupidly hadn't taken into account—the powerful sense of recognition at seeing him. The sense of familiarity, even though this man was little more than a stranger to her.

Because here was Alex in adulthood, she realised shakily—or rather, here was a version of what Alex *could* become. Strong, powerful, prosperous. And wasn't that what every mother wanted for her son? A lion of a man, as opposed to a sheep.

Whereas the Alex she had left back at home being looked after by a frankly cynical Sarah—well, that Alex was headed in a completely different direction. Bullied at school and living a life where every penny mattered and was counted—how could he possibly achieve his true potential like that? What kind of a future was she offering him?

And any last, lingering doubt that she must be crazy to even contemplate a scheme like this withered away in that instant. Because she owed Alex this.

It didn't matter if her pride was hurt or the last of her

stupid, romantic memories of her time with Constantine was crushed into smithereens—she owed her son this.

But as Laura approached him again, it was difficult not to react to him on so many different levels. His had always been an imposing presence, but the passing of the years seemed to have magnified his potent charisma. There had been no softening of the hard, muscular body—nor dimming of the golden luminance of his skin. And, while there might be a lick of silver at his temples, his wavy dark hair was as thick as ever. But with age had come a certain cool distance which had not been there before. He carried about him the unmistakable aura of the magnate—a man with power radiating from every atom of his expensively clad frame.

Laura felt the erratic fluttering of her heart. Yet none of that mattered. His eyes were still the blackest she had ever seen, and his lips remained a study in sensuality. She still sensed that here was a man in the truest sense of the word—all elemental passion and hunger beneath the sophisticated exterior.

'Your water, sir,' she said, trying to curve her mouth into a friendly smile and silently praying that he would return it.

Hadn't he once told her that her smile was like the sun coming out? Wouldn't that stir some distant memory in his mind? And didn't they say something about the voice always striking a note of recognition—that people changed but their voices never did?

She spoke the longest sentence possible under the circumstances. 'I…I wasn't sure if you wanted still or sparkling, sir—so I've brought both. They both come from…from the Cotswolds!' she added wildly, noticing the label. A fact from a recent early-morning farming programme on the radio came flooding back to her. 'It's…um…filtered through the oolitic limestone of the Cotswold Hills, and you won't find a purer water anywhere!'

'How fascinating,' murmured Constantine sardonically, taking one of the glasses from the tray and wondering why she sounded as if she was advertising the brand. She didn't *look* like the kind of out-of-work actress who would moonlight as a waitress, but you could never be sure. 'Thanks.'

He gave a curt nod and, turning his back on her, walked away without another word and Laura was left staring at him, her heart pounding with fear and frustration. But what had she expected? That he would engage her in some small-talk which would provide the perfect opportunity for her to tell him he had a son? Start remarking that the slice of lemon which was bobbing around in his glass of fizzy water was vastly inferior to the lemons he grew on his very own Greek island?

No. The smile hadn't worked and neither had the voice. Those black eyes had not widened in growing comprehension, and he had not shaken his coal-dark head to say, in a tone of disbelief and admiration, *Why, you're the young English virgin I had the most amazing sex with all those years ago! Do you know that not a day goes by when I don't think about you?*

Laura chewed on her lip. Fantasies never worked out the way you planned them, did they? And fantasies were dangerous. She mustn't allow herself to indulge in them just because she had never really got over their one night together. She was just going to have to choose her moment carefully—because she wasn't leaving this building without Constantine Karantinos being in full possession of all the facts.

* * *

The evening passed in a blur of activity—but at least being busy stopped her from getting too anxious about the prospect which lay ahead.

There had been a lavish sit-down dinner for three hundred people, though the space beside Constantine had remained glaringly empty. It must be for his girlfriend, thought Laura painfully. So where was she? Why wasn't she sticking like glue to the side of the handsome Greek who was talking so carelessly to the women in a tiara on the other side of him. *It was a royal princess!* Laura realised. Hadn't she recently come out of a high-profile divorce and walked away with a record-breaking settlement?

Laura had managed to pass right by him with a dish of chocolates, just in time to hear the Princess inviting him to stay on her yacht later that summer—but Constantine had merely shrugged his broad shoulders and murmured something about his diary being full.

The candlelight caught the jewels which were strung around the neck of every woman present—so that the whole room seemed to be glittering. In the background, the harpist had calmed down, and was now working his way through a serene medley of tunes.

It was not just a different world, Laura realised as she carried out yet another tray of barely touched food back to the kitchens, it was like a completely alien *universe*. She thought of the savings she had to make so that Alex would have a nice Christmas, and shuddered to think how much this whole affair must be costing—why, the wine budget alone would have been more than the amount she lived on in a single year. And Constantine was paying for it all. For him it would be no more than a drop in the ocean.

The guests had now all moved into the ballroom, where the harpist had been replaced by a band, and people had started dancing. But the minutes were melting by without Laura getting anywhere near Constantine, let alone close enough to be able to talk to him. People were clustering around him like flies, and it was getting on for midnight. Soon the party would end and she'd be sent home—and then what?

There was a momentary lull before a conversational buzz began to hum around the ballroom, and then the dancing crowd stilled and parted as a woman began to slowly sashay through them, with all the panache of someone whose job it was to be gazed at by other people. Her flaxen fall of hair guaranteed instant attention, as did the ice-blue eyes and willowy limbs which seemed to sum up her cool and unattainable beauty.

She wore a dazzling white fur stole draped over a silver dress, and at over six feet tall she dominated the room like the tallest of bright poppies. And there was really only one person in the room who was man enough not to be dwarfed by her impressive height—the man she was headed for as unerringly as a comet crashing towards earth.

'It's Ingrid Johansson,' Laura heard someone say, and then, 'Isn't she *gorgeous*?'

Convulsively, she felt her fingers clutching at her apron as she watched the blonde goddess slink up to Constantine and place a proprietorial hand on his forearm before leaning forward to kiss him on each cheek.

Constantine was aware of everyone watching them as Ingrid leaned forward to kiss him. 'That was quite an entrance,' he murmured, but inside he felt the first faint flicker of disdain.

'Was it?' Ingrid looked into his eyes with an expression of mock-innocence. 'Must we stay here, *alskling*? I'm so tired.'

'No,' Constantine said evenly. 'We don't have to stay here at all—we can go upstairs to my suite.'

To Laura's horror she saw the couple begin to move towards the door, and she felt her forehead break out into a cold sweat.

Now what?

She saw some of the bulkier security men begin to follow them, and the slightly disappointed murmur from the rest of the guests as they began to realise that the star attractions were leaving. Soon Constantine would be swallowed up by the same kind of protection which had shielded him so effectively from her all those years ago...

And then a terrible thought occurred to her—a dark thought which came from nowhere and which had never even blipped on her radar before. Or maybe she had simply never allowed it to. What if it *hadn't* been his security people who had kept her away from him all those years ago? What if he'd *known* that she was trying to make contact? And what if he'd actually *read* the letter she'd sent, telling him about Alex, and had decided to ignore it?

What if he had simply *chosen not to have anything to do with his own son*?

A cold, sick feeling of dread made her skin suddenly clammy, but Laura knew it was a chance she had to take. If that had been the case, then maybe she would find out about it now. And if he chose to reject his son again...well, then she wanted to see his face while he did it.

She went over to the bar and ordered a bottle of the most expensive champagne and two glasses.

'Put it on Mr Karantinos's account,' she said recklessly,

and took the tray away before the barman could query why the order hadn't gone through room service.

Her flat, sensible shoes made no sound as they squished across the marble foyer, but within the mirror-lined walls of the lift she was confronted with the reality of her appearance and she shuddered. Hair scraped back into a tight bun, on top of which was perched a ridiculous little frilly cap. A plain black dress hung unflatteringly over her knees and was topped with a white-frilled apron.

She looked like a throwback to another age, when people in the service industry really *were* servants. Laura was used to wearing a uniform in the bread shop—what she was not used to was looking like some kind of haunted and out-of-place ghost of a woman. A woman who must now go and face one of the world's most noted beauties, who happened to be sharing a bed with a man whose child Laura had borne.

The lift glided upwards and stopped with smooth silence at the penthouse suite, its doors sliding open to reveal Laura's worst fears. Two dark and burly-looking men were standing guard outside the door. So now what? Fixing on a confident smile, which contradicted the awful nerves which were twisting her stomach like writhing snakes, Laura walked towards the door.

One of the guards raised his eyebrows. 'Where do you think you're going?'

His accent was thickly Greek, and somehow it only added tension to her already jangled nerves. Laura's smile widened, though a bead of sweat was trickling its way slowly down her back. 'Champagne for Mr Karantinos.'

'He told us he didn't want to be disturbed.'

Because of what was at stake, Laura found herself

digging deep inside herself, finding courage where she had expected to find fear. Her smile became conspiratorial; she even managed a wink. 'I think he's about to announce his engagement,' she whispered.

The other guard shrugged and jerked his head in the direction of the door. 'Go on, then.'

Rapping loudly on the door, Laura heard a muffled exclamation—but she knew she couldn't turn back now. She had to get this over with—because if she left it much longer she might find them...find them...

Blocking out the unbearable thought of Constantine and the supermodel beginning to make love, Laura pushed open the door, and the scene before her stamped itself on her gaze like a bizarre tableau.

There was Constantine, staring hard at the supermodel. And there was Ingrid staring back at him, her expression disbelieving. She had removed her fur wrap, and her dress was nothing but a sliver of silver which clung to her body and revealed the points of her nipples.

They both looked round as she walked in.

'What the hell do you think you are doing?' demanded Constantine, and then frowned as he saw the tray she was carrying. 'You don't just walk into my suite like this—and I didn't order champagne.'

Not even he was cold-hearted enough to celebrate the fact that he'd just finished with his girlfriend—even though Ingrid was still standing there staring at him as if she didn't quite believe it.

Putting the tray down on a table before she dropped it, Laura looked up at him, her voice low and trembling. 'I need to talk to you.' She glanced over at the model, who was glaring at her. 'Alone, if that's all right.'

'Who the hell is this?' snapped Ingrid.

He had absolutely no idea, and for one moment Constantine wondered if the insipid little waitress was some kind of set-up. Were her male accomplices about to burst in with cameras? Or did her uniform conceal some kind of weapon? Hadn't kidnap attempts been suspected enough times in the past?

But he remembered her from the ballroom—her pinched, pale face and her inappropriate babbling on about some type of water. She didn't look like the kind of woman capable of any kind of elaborate subterfuge. And her expression was peculiar; he had never seen a woman look quite like that before—and it made him study her more closely.

Her cheeks were pale but her grey eyes were huge, and she looked as if she was fighting to control her breathing. Her breasts—surprisingly pert breasts for such a tiny frame, he thought inconsequentially—were heaving like someone who had just dragged themselves out of the water after nearly drowning.

'Who are you?' he demanded hotly. 'And what do you want?'

'I told you,' answered Laura quietly. 'I need to talk to you. Alone, if I may.'

Constantine's eyes narrowed as some primeval instinct urged him to listen to what this woman was saying. And something in her strange urgency told him to ensure that they had no audience. He turned to the supermodel, praying that she wouldn't make the kind of scene which some women revelled in when a man had just ended a relationship.

'I think you'd better leave now, don't you, Ingrid?' he questioned quietly. 'I have a car which will take you wherever you want to go.'

For a moment Laura felt eaten up with guilt and shame as she saw the supermodel's stricken face, and her heart went out to her. Because what woman wouldn't be able to identify with the terrible battle taking place within the gorgeous blonde? Anyone could see she wanted to stay—but it was also easy to see from the obdurate and cold expression on Constantine's face that he wanted the supermodel out of there.

Oh, this was just terrible—and it was all her fault. Awkwardly, she shifted from one foot to the other. 'Look, perhaps I can…come back.'

'*You* are not going anywhere,' snapped Constantine as he flicked her a hard glance. 'Ingrid was just leaving.'

At this, Ingrid's mouth thinned into a scarlet line. 'You *bastard*,' she hissed, and marched out of the suite without another word.

For a moment there was silence, and Laura's heart was pounding with fear and disbelief as she lifted up her hands in a gesture of apology. 'I'm sorry—'

'Shut up,' he snapped, two fists clenching by the shafts of his powerful thighs as a quiet fury continued to spiral up inside him. 'And don't give me any misplaced sentiments. Do you think you can hysterically burst in here making veiled threats and then act like a concerned and responsible citizen who cares about the havoc she's wreaked along the way? Do you?'

Nervously, Laura sank her teeth into her bottom lip. She supposed she deserved that—just as she supposed she had no choice other than to stand there and take it. Maybe if she let him vent his anger then he would calm down, and they could sit down afterwards and talk calmly.

His black eyes bored into her like fierce black lasers. 'So

who *are* you?' he continued furiously. 'And why are you really here?'

Brushing aside her hurt that he *still* didn't recognise her, Laura tried again. 'I…' It sounded so bizarre to say it now that the moment had arrived. To say these words of such import to a man who was staring at her so forbiddingly. But then Alex's face swam into the forefront of her mind, and suddenly it was easy.

She drew a deep breath. 'I'm sorry it has to be this way, but I've come to tell you that seven years ago I had a baby. Your baby.' Her voice shaking with emotion, she got the final words out in a rush. 'You have a son, Constantine, and I am the mother of that son.'

CHAPTER THREE

CONSTANTINE stared at the trembling waitress who stood before him, and who had just made such a preposterous claim. That *she* was the mother of *his* son. Why, it would almost be laughable were it not so outrageous.

'That is a bizarre and untrue statement to make,' he snapped. 'Especially since I don't even know you.'

Laura felt as if he had plunged a stiletto into her heart, but she prayed it didn't show on her face. 'Then why didn't you have the guards take me away?'

'Because I'm curious.'

'Or because you know that deep down I could be telling the truth?'

'Not in this case.' His lips curved into a cruel smile. 'You see, I don't screw around with waitresses.'

It hurt. Oh, how it hurt—but presumably that had been his intention. Laura forced herself not to hit back at the slur, nor to let herself wither under his blistering gaze. 'Maybe you don't now—but I can assure you that wasn't always the case.'

Something in her calm certainty—in the way she stood there, facing up to him, despite her cheap clothes and lowly demeanour—all those things combined to make Constantine consider the bizarre possibility of her words. That they might be *true*. He looked deep into her eyes, as if searching for some hint of what this was all about, but all he saw was the stormy distress lurking in their pewter depths, and suddenly he felt his heart lurch. Eyes like storm clouds.

Storm clouds.

Another memory stirred deep in the recesses of his mind. 'Take down your hair,' he ordered softly.

'But—'

'I said, take down your hair.'

Compelled by the silken urgency of his voice, and weakened by the derision in his eyes, Laura reached up her hand. First, off came the frilly little cap, which she let fall to the floor—she certainly wouldn't be needing *that* again. Then, with trembling fingers, she began to remove the pins and finally the elastic band.

It was a relief to be free of the tight restraints and she shook her hair completely loose, only vaguely aware of Constantine's sudden inrush of breath.

He watched as lock after lock fell free—one silken fall of moon-pale hair after another. Fine hair, but masses of it. Hair which had looked like a dull, mediocre cap now took on the gleaming lustre of honey and sand as it tumbled over her slight shoulders. Her face was still pale—and the dark grey eyes looked huge.

Storm clouds, he thought again, as more memories began to filter through, like a picture slowly coming into focus.

A small English harbour. A summer spent unencumbered by the pressures of the family business. And a need to escape from Greece around the time of the anniversary of his mother's death—a time when his father became unbearably maudlin, even though it had been many years since she had died.

His father had promised him far more responsibility in the Karantinos shipping business, and that summer Constantine had recognised that soon he would no longer be able to go off on the annual month-long sailing holiday he loved so much. That this might be the last chance he would get for a true taste of freedom. And he'd been right. Later that summer he'd gone back to Greece and been given access to the company's accounts for the first time— only to discover with rising disbelief just how dire the state of the family finances was. And just how much his father had neglected the business in his obsessive grief for his late wife.

It had been the last trip where he was truly young. Shrugging off routine, and shrugging on his oldest jeans, Constantine had sailed around the Mediterranean as the mood took him, lapping up the sun and feeling all the tension gradually leave his body. He hadn't wanted women—there were always women if he wanted them—he had wanted peace. So he'd read books. Slept. Swum. Fished.

As the days had gone by his olive skin had become darker. His black hair had grown longer, the waves curling around the nape of his neck so that he had looked like some kind of ancient buccaneer. He'd sailed around England to explore the place properly—something he'd always meant to do ever since an English teacher had read him stories about her country. He'd wanted to see the improbable world of castles and green fields come alive.

And eventually he'd anchored at the little harbour of Milmouth and found a cute hotel which looked as if it had been lifted straight out of the set of a period drama. Little old ladies had been sitting eating cream cakes on a wonderful emerald lawn as he strolled across it, wearing a faded

pair of jeans and a T-shirt. Several of the old ladies had
gawped as he'd pulled out a chair at one of the empty tables
and then spread his long legs out in front of him. Cream
cakes which had been heading for mouths had never quite
reached their destination and had been discarded—but then
he often had that effect on women, no matter what their age.

And then a waitress had come walking across the grass
towards him and Constantine's eyes had narrowed. There
hadn't been anything particularly *special* about her—and
yet there had been something about her clear, pale skin and
the youthful vigour of her step which had caught his attention and his desire. Something familiar and yet unknown
had stirred deep within him. The crumpled petals of her lips
had demanded to be kissed. And she'd had beautiful eyes,
so deep and grey—a pewter colour he'd only ever seen
before in angry seas or storm clouds. It had been—what?
Weeks since he had had a woman? And suddenly he'd
wanted her. Badly.

'I'm afraid you can't sit there,' she said softly, as her
shadow fell over him.

'Can't?' Even her mild officiousness was turning him
on—as was the pure, clean tone of her accent. He looked
up, narrowing his eyes against the sun. 'Why not?'

'Because…because I'm afraid the management have a
rule about no jeans being allowed.'

'But I'm hungry,' he murmured. 'Very hungry.' He gave
her a slow smile as he looked her up and down. 'So what
do you suggest?'

As a recipient of that careless smile, the girl was like
putty in his hands. She suggested serving him tea at an
unseen side of the hotel, by a beautiful little copse of trees.
Giggling, she smuggled out sandwiches, and scones with

jam and something he'd never eaten before nor since, called clotted cream. And when she finished work she agreed to have dinner with him. Her name was Laura and it made him think of laurels and the fresh green garlands which ancient Greeks wore on their heads to protect them. She was sweet—very sweet—and it was a long time since he'd held a woman in his arms.

The outcome of the night was predictable—but her reaction wasn't. Unlike the wealthy sophisticates he usually associated with, she played no games with him. She had a vulnerability about her which she wasn't afraid of showing. But Constantine always ran a million miles from vulnerability—even though her pink and white body and her grey eyes lured him into her arms like a siren.

In the morning she didn't want to let him go—but of course he had to leave. He was Constantine Karantinos—heir to one of the mightiest shipping dynasties in the whole of Greece—and his destiny was not to stay in the arms of a small-town waitress.

How strange the memory could be, thought Constantine—as the images faded and he found himself emerging into real-time, standing in a luxury London penthouse with that same waitress standing trembling-lipped in front of him and telling him she had conceived a child that night. And how random fate could be, he thought bitterly, to bring such a woman back into his life—and with such earth-shattering news.

He walked over to the drinks cabinet and poured himself a tumbler of water—more as a delaying tactic than anything else. 'Do you want anything?' he questioned, still with his back to her.

Laura thought that a drink might choke her. 'No.'

He drank the water and then turned round. Her face looked chalk-white, and something nagged at him to tell her to sit down—but his anger and his indignation were stronger than his desire to care for a woman who had just burst into his life making such claims as these.

A son....

'I wore protection that night,' he stated coldly.

Laura flinched. How clinical he sounded. But there was no use in her having pointless yearnings about how different his reaction might have been. She knew that fantasies didn't come true. Try to imagine yourself in his shoes, she urged herself. A woman he barely knew, coming back into his life with the most momentous and presumably unwelcome news of all.

'Obviously it failed to do what it was supposed to do,' she said, her voice as matter-of-fact as she could make it.

'And this child is you say...how old?'

'He's seven.'

He felt the slam of his heart and an unwelcome twist of his gut. Constantine turned and stared out of the vast windows which overlooked the darkened park before the unwanted emotions could show on his face. A son! Above the shadowed shapes of the trees he could see the faint glimmer of stars and for a moment he thought about the stars, back home, which burned as brightly as lanterns. Then just as suddenly he turned back again, his now composed gaze raking over her white face, searching for truth in the smoky splendour of her eyes.

'So why didn't you tell me this before?' he demanded. 'Why wait seven long years? Why now?'

Laura opened her mouth to explain that she'd tried, but before she had a chance to answer him she saw his black eyes narrow with cynical understanding.

'Ah, yes, but of course,' he said softly. 'Of course. It was the perfect moment, wasn't it?'

Laura frowned. 'I don't know what you're—'

But her thoughts on the matter were obviously super-fluous, for ruthlessly he cut through her words as if he were wielding a guillotine. 'You wait long enough to ensure that I can have no influence—even if the child *is* mine. How is it that the old saying goes? *Give me a child until he is seven and I shall give you the man.*' He took a step towards her, his posture as menacing as the silken threat in his voice. 'So what happened? Did you read the papers and hear that that Karantinos stock has soared, and then decide that this was the optimum time to strike? Did you think that coming out with this piece of information now would put you in a strong bargaining position?'

'*B-bargaining* position?' echoed Laura in disbelief. He might have been talking about a plot of land…when this was their *son* they were discussing.

His voice was as steely cold as his eyes. 'I don't know why you're affecting outrage,' he clipped out. 'I presume you want money?'

Automatically, Laura reached her hand out and steadied herself on a giant sofa—afraid that her trembling knees might give way but determined not to sit down. Because that would surely put her in an even weaker position—if she had to sit looking up at him like a child who had been put on the naughty chair. But even her protest sounded deflated. 'How dare you say that?' she whispered.

'Well, why else are you here if you haven't come looking for a hand-out?'

'I don't have to stay here and listen to your insults.'

'Oh, but I am afraid that you do. You aren't going

anywhere,' he said with silky menace as he glittered her a brittle look. 'Until we get this thing sorted out.'

This thing happened to be their son, thought Laura— until she realised with a pang that maybe the Greek's angry words had the ring of truth to them. Because Alex was *her* son, not his. Constantine had never been a part of his life. *And maybe he never would be.* For a moment she felt a wave of guilt as Constantine's black gaze pierced through her like a sabre.

'Just by telling me you have involved me—like it or not,' he continued remorselessly as his gaze burned into her. 'Didn't you realise that every action has consequences?'

'You think I don't know that better than anyone?' she retorted, stung.

Something in her response renewed the slam of his heart against his ribcage, and Constantine narrowed his eyes, searching for every possible flaw in her argument the way he had learnt to do at work—an ability that had made him a formidable legend within the world of international shipping. 'So why didn't you tell me about this before— like seven years ago?'

She still wanted to turn and run, but she doubted that her feet would obey her brain's command to walk, let alone run. 'I tried...' She saw the scorn on his face. 'Yes, I tried! I tried tracking you down—but you weren't especially easy to trace.'

'Because I hadn't meant it to be anything more than a one-night stand!' he roared, steeling himself against the distressed crumpling of her lips.

'Then don't you talk to *me* about consequences,' she whispered.

There was a pause as he watched her struggling to

control her breathing, her grey eyes almost black with distress. 'So what happened?' he persisted.

Laura sucked in a low, shuddering breath. 'I managed to find out the address and phone number of your headquarters in Athens.' She had been completely gobsmacked to discover that her scruffy jeans-wearing, slightly maverick Greek lover turned out to be someone very important in some huge shipping company. 'I tried ringing, but no one would put me through—and I sent you a letter, but it obviously never reached you. And I've tried several times since then.'

Usually around the time of her son's birthday, when Alex would start asking questions, making her long to be able to introduce the little boy to his father.

'The result has always been the same,' she finished bitterly. 'It doesn't matter how I've broached it or what approach I've made—every time I've failed to even get a phone call with you.'

Constantine was silent for a moment as he considered her words, for now he could imagine exactly what must have happened. An unknown English girl ringing and asking to be put through to Kyrios Constantine—why, she would have been swatted away as if she were a troublesome fly buzzing over a plate of food. Likewise any letters. They would have been opened and scrutinised. Who would have made the decision not to show him? he wondered, and then sighed, for this was something he *could* believe.

The ancient Greek troop formation of a tightly-knit and protective group known as the phalanx still existed in modern Greece, Constantine thought wryly. It was not the right of his workers to shield him, but he could see exactly why they had done it. Women had always shamelessly pursued him—how were his staff to have known that this woman might actually have had a case. *Might*, he reminded himself. Only *might*.

There was a pause. 'Do you have a photo?' he demanded. 'Of the child?'

Laura nodded, swallowing down her relief. At last! And surely asking to see a picture of Alex was a good sign? Wouldn't he set eyes on his gorgeous black-eyed son and know in an instant that there could only be one possible father? 'It's…it's in my handbag—downstairs in the staff cloakroom. Shall I go and get it?'

He was strangely reluctant to let her out of his sight. As if she might disappear off into the night and he would never see her again. *But wouldn't that be the ideal scenario?* The question came out of nowhere, but Constantine pushed it away. He stared down into those deep grey eyes and inexplicably his mouth dried. 'I'll come with you.'

'But I'll…'

Black brows were raised. 'You'll what?'

She had been about to say that she would be sacked if she were seen strolling through the hotel with one of the guests—but, come to think of it, it wasn't as if she was planning to work here again. 'People will talk,' she said. 'If you're seen accompanying one of the waitresses to the staff cloakroom.'

'So let them talk,' he snapped. 'I think it is a little late in the day for you to act concerned after your dramatic entrance into my suite!' And he pulled open the door and stalked out, leaving Laura to follow while he spoke in rapid Greek to the two guards.

They rode down in the penthouse lift, which seemed to have shrunk in dimension since the last time she had been in it. Laura was acutely aware of his proximity and the way his powerful frame seemed to dominate the small space. She was close enough to see the silken gleam of his skin and to breathe in that heady masculine tang which was all his. Close enough to touch…

And Constantine knew that she was aware of him; he could sense it in the sudden shallowness of her breathing— the way a pulse began fluttering wildly beneath the fine skin at her temple. Did she desire him now, as women always did, and was anger responsible for the answering call in his own body? The sudden thick heat at his groin? The furious desire to open her legs and bring her right up against him, so that he could thrust deep into her body and spill out some of his rage? What was it about this plain little thing which should suddenly have him in such a torrent of longing?

He swallowed down the sudden unbearable dryness in his throat as the lift came to a halt and the door slid open on some subterranean level of the hotel he hadn't known existed. Laura began to lead the way through a maze of corridors until she reached the women's cloakroom.

'Wait here,' she said breathlessly.

But he reached out and levered her chin upwards with the tips of his fingers, feeling her tremble as he captured her troubled gaze with the implacable spotlight of his own.

'Don't run away, will you?' he murmured, with silky menace.

Laura stilled. In the light of all the vicious accusations he had hurled at her, his touch should have repelled her— but it did no such thing. To her horror, it reminded her of what it was like to be touched by a man, and the hard, seeking certainty of this man's particular touch.

With an effort she jerked her head away. 'I wasn't pl-planning to.'

'Hurry up,' he ordered, as the heat at his groin intensi-fied—for he had seen the sudden darkening of her eyes and sensed her body's instinctive desire for him. That in itself was nothing new—women always desired him—what perplexed him was the answering hunger which stirred in his blood.

Laura nodded. 'I…I can't stay in this uniform. I'd better change while I'm in there—so I may be a couple of minutes.'

'I'll wait,' he ground out, but her words triggered an unwanted series of explicit and strangely powerful memories as the door closed behind her. Of the young woman who had shed her clothes with such unashamed pleasure—taking him into her pink and white body and gasping out her pleasure. Had that same woman conceived his child that night? he found himself asking, the question spinning round and round in his brain as he stared at the dingy wall of the staff corridor.

Laura took off her uniform and, leaving it neatly folded beside one of the laundry baskets, she pulled on her jeans, T-shirt and thin jumper—she'd experienced too many cold winters not to have learnt the benefits of layering. Then she picked up her handbag and waterproof jacket and walked outside, to where Constantine stood in exactly the same spot, like a daunting dark statue.

Beneath the harsh glare of the overhead light, she began delving around in her handbag until she pulled out the picture of Alex taken at school, just a few months ago—she handed it to him.

Constantine stared down at it in silence for a long moment. The child had black eyes and a faint olive tint to his skin, and the dark curls of his hair looked as if an attempt had been made to tame them especially for the photo—but already they were beginning to escape. He remembered his own hair being just as stubborn at such an age.

Narrowing his eyes, he studied the image more carefully. The child was smiling, yes—but there was an unmistakable wariness about that smile, and Constantine felt a sudden wild leap of protectiveness, mixed in with an innate sense of denial. As if the logical side of his mind refused to accept that he could start the evening by hosting a glittering party and then the evening would end with a paternity claim foisted on him out of the blue. That he should suddenly be a father. He shook his head.

'He looks just like you!' Laura blurted out, wanting him to say something—anything—to break this tense and awful silence.

An icy feeling chilled his skin. He had never felt quite so out of control as he now found himself—not since his mother had died and he had watched his father fall to pieces before his eyes, and had decided there and then that love did dangerous things to a man. 'Does he?'

'Oh, yes.'

'That proves nothing,' he snarled as he thrust the photograph back into her hand. 'For all I know this might just be a very clever scam.'

Laura swayed, unable to believe that he would think her so cold and calculating. So *manipulative.* So sexually free and easy. But why shouldn't he think that? He didn't know her—just as she didn't know him. Though the more of himself he revealed, the more she was beginning to dislike him. Had he forgotten that she had gone into his arms an innocent, unable to resist the powerful sexual pull he had exerted?

'B-but you knew that I was a virgin that night,' she reminded him painfully.

He shrugged, as if her words meant nothing—but the concept of a woman's purity was both potent and important to a man as traditional as Constantine. He forced himself to remember his incredulity that a young woman should so casually give her virginity to a man she knew she would never see again. Or had *he* been naïve? With her he had played the man he had never allowed himself to be— the itinerant traveller without a care in the world. What if her sweet and supposed ignorance of his wealth and his status had all been an act? Suppose she'd seen his yacht and started asking questions in between serving him tea and having dinner with him? Wouldn't that make her eagerness to lose her innocence to a man who was little more than a stranger more understandable?

Constantine had spent his whole life being surrounded by people who wanted something from him—maybe this woman was no different.

'You *told* me you were a virgin, but those could have simply been words. And, yes, I know that you gasped as I entered you,' he said brutally, before pausing to add a final, painful boast. 'But women always do—maybe it is something to do with my size, or my technique.' He shrugged as her fingertips flew to her lips, hardening his heart against her obvious distress. 'Maybe you thought that affecting purity would guarantee you some sort of future with the kind of man you were unlikely to meet again. That if I thought you were a virgin I would think more highly of you—rather than just as a woman who had casual sex with a man she'd just met.'

Laura felt ill. It was as if he had taken her memories of

the past and ground them to dust beneath his heel. 'Well, if you think that,' she said, putting the photo back in her wallet with trembling fingers, 'then there's nothing more to be said, is there?'

But Constantine moved closer, so close that she could feel his body heat, and she hated the thought that flashed through her mind without warning. This was the man who had planted a seed in her body...whose child had grown within her. The image was so overwhelming that it made her instinctively shudder. And wasn't nature famously canny, if cruel—conditioning women to desire the biological father of their child, even if that man was utterly heartless? Laura swallowed, because now he was lowering his head towards her so that she was caught in the intense ebony blaze of his eyes. Surely he wasn't going to...?

But he was.

He caught her against him, crushing her tiny frame against his and enfolding her within his powerful arms. She could feel the fierce hard heat of his body where it touched hers, and knew that she should cry out her protest—but she could no sooner stop this than she could have stopped the earth spinning around the sun.

His mouth came down to capture hers, and even though Laura was desperately inexperienced when it came to men she could sense the simmering anger which lay behind his kiss. This was a kiss which had more to do with anger than desire. But that didn't stop her responding to it—didn't stop her body flaring up with desire as if he had just ignited it with some hidden fuse. *He despises me,* was her last sane thought as the expert touch of his mouth made her lips part willingly beneath his.

His hands were tight around her waist and her own were

splayed over the hard chest, where she could feel the rapid thundering of his heart. And through the kiss Laura made a little sound of disbelief—wondering how she could respond with such melting pleasure to a man who clearly viewed her with utter contempt.

The sound seemed to startle him, for just as suddenly as he had taken her in his arms he let her go, so that she had to steady herself against the wall as she stared up at him.

'Wh-what was that all about?' she breathed.

What, indeed? With an effort, Constantine controlled his ragged breathing and stared at her, shaking his head as if to deny the intensity of that kiss. It had been all about desire, he told himself fiercely—a powerful desire which was no respecter of circumstance or status. And how extraordinary that he should feel such overwhelming lust for this washed-out little waitress. Inappropriate, too—when to do so would surely weaken his case against her preposterous claim.

He looked down at her, his heart pounding so powerfully in his chest and his groin so hard with need that for a moment he couldn't think straight. 'You will need to get a DNA test done as quickly as possible,' he grated.

Laura's eyes widened in distress. 'But... But...'

'But what?' he cut in scornfully, and gave a short laugh as the aftermath of the kiss faded and reality flashed in like a sharp knife. 'Did you really think that I was going to acknowledge the boy as a Karantinos heir—giving him access to one of the world's greatest fortunes—simply because you say so and because the boy bears a passing resemblance to me?'

'But you—'

'Yes, he looks Greek,' he finished witheringly. 'But for

all I know you might be one of those women who turn on for Greek men.' He gave a blistering smile as his gaze raked over her kiss-swollen lips. 'I think you've just demonstrated that to both our satisfaction.'

Laura slumped back against the wall and stared up at him. Was that why he had kissed her—to make her look morally loose? And then to follow it up with a cold-blooded demand that she prove Alex was his child? 'Why, you…you *bastard*!' she gasped.

Constantine reflected that women were remarkably unimaginative when it came to insults. And didn't they realise that *they* were the ones who put themselves into situations which gave men ammunition to criticise them?

But inside he was hurting for reasons he wasn't even close to understanding—a state of being so rare for him that it made him want to hurt back, and badly.

'I should be careful about my choice of words, if I were you, Laura,' he informed her coldly. 'It isn't *my* parentage which is in doubt. If tests prove that the boy is mine, then I will take responsibility—but first you're going to have to prove it.'

CHAPTER FOUR

'WHAT do you mean, he wants a DNA test?'

Laura stared at her sister, trying to snap out of the terrible sense of weariness which seemed to have settled over her like a dank cloud. After leaving the Granchester last night she had spent a few restless hours in a cheap London hotel before catching the first train back to Milmouth—her mind still spinning with all the hurtful things Constantine had said to her. On the plus side, she had arrived back in time to take Alex to school, but now she was back in the shop, Sarah having coped with the morning rush of customers. This quiet spell meant that Laura was now forced to face Sarah's furious interrogation.

She shrugged her shoulders listlessly—she had gone through every emotion from anger and indignation through to sheer humiliation and had worn herself out with them. 'It's fairly self-explanatory, isn't it? He wants a DNA test done. He wants proof that Alex is his son.'

'Did you show him the photo?'

'Of course I did.'

'And?'

There was a pause while Laura thought about how best to put it, strangely reluctant to repeat Constantine's wounding words. Was it her own hurt pride which stopped her from telling her sister how much he clearly despised her and all she stood for? 'He said that although Alex looked Greek he couldn't possibly risk acknowledging an heir to such a vast fortune as his without proof.'

'The bastard!'

And even though she'd hurled exactly the same word at him last night, Laura now found herself in the bizarre position of putting forward a contrary point of view. One that she had been thinking about during her early morning train journey. 'I can see his point,' she said carefully. 'I mean, he doesn't know that he's the only possible contender who could be Alex's father, does he?'

'Didn't you tell him?'

'No.' His anger had been too palpable; the mood between them too volatile. Why, he'd even accused her of using her virginity as a bargaining tool. 'And even if I had he might not have believed me. Why should he?'

Sarah frowned. 'Laura—I don't believe this! You're not *defending* him, are you?'

'Of course I'm not,' replied Laura stiffly.

But the truth was far more complex. She *could* see Constantine's point—even though it hurt her to the core that he should think her capable of having lots of partners and just wanting to foist paternity on the richest candidate. The way she had acted the day she'd met him had been uncharacteristic behaviour she'd never repeated—but Constantine wasn't to know that, was he?

'For all he knows, there might have been a long line of Greek lovers in my life,' she told her sister fiercely, blinking furiously to stop the rogue tears from pricking at her eyes.

'What? All of them sailing their yachts into Milmouth?'

questioned Sarah sarcastically. 'I didn't realise our town was twinned with Athens!'

'Very funny,' said Laura as she pulled on her apron.

But at least Sarah's acerbic comments had helped focus her mind, and she went on the internet at lunchtime—cursing the dyslexia which made her progress slow as she laboriously pored over websites which offered information about DNA-testing. Sitting in the cramped little corner of the sitting room where they kept the computer, she studied it until she was certain she knew all the facts—and she was startled by the sudden sound of her cellphone ringing. She used it mainly for emergencies—only a few people had the number—and this was one she didn't recognise.

But the voice she did. Instantly.

'Laura?'

Briefly, she closed her eyes. Away from the cruel spotlight of his eyes, it was all too easy to let the honeyed gravel of Constantine's faintly accented voice wash over her. It tugged at her senses, whispering over her suddenly goosebumpy skin, reminding her of just how good a man's kiss could make a woman's starved senses feel.

Appalled at the inappropriate path of her thoughts—especially when he was forcing Alex to go through the indignity of a DNA test—Laura sat up straight and glared at the computer screen. Get real, she told herself furiously.

'Hello, Constantine.'

'Ah, you recognised my voice,' he observed softly.

'Funny that, isn't it? Yet, strange as it may seem, there aren't scores of Greek men growling down the telephone at me.'

Detecting a distinctively spiky note in her voice, Constantine frowned. Was she daring to be sarcastic—to *him*? And under such circumstances, too? 'You know why I'm calling?'

'Yes.'

'You will agree to the DNA test?'

Laura gripped the phone tightly. What choice did she have? 'I suppose so.'

'Good.' Leaning back in the sumptuous leather of his chair, Constantine surveyed the broad spectrum of the glittering London skyline. 'I've been making some enquiries and I can either arrange for you to have it done at my lawyer's office here in London—or he tells me that he can arrange for you to use somewhere closer to you, if that's more convenient.'

She heard an unexpected note of silky persuasion in his voice, and suddenly Laura was glad that she had done her research, glad that she wasn't just going to accept what the powerful and autocratic Greek was telling her. *What it was in his best interests to tell her.*

'I'm not using a lawyer's office,' she said quietly.

There was a disbelieving pause. 'Why not?'

'Because I believe that doing so carries all kinds of legal implications,' she said. 'This test is being done to establish paternity to your satisfaction; it is not a custody claim. So I'm doing the test at home on a purely need-to-know basis.'

Another pause, longer this time. Constantine had not been expecting her to query his wishes—to be honest, he had expected her simply to accept his agenda. Because people always did; they bowed to the dominance of his will. So just who did this mousy little waitress think she was to dare to oppose his wishes? He lowered his voice. 'And if I object?'

'You aren't in any position to object!' she declared, refusing to let that silky tone intimidate her. 'You're the one who wants this damned test—who is going to force me to take a swab from my seven-year-old son's mouth. Have you thought what I'm going to tell him? How I'm going to explain *that* to a seven-year-old boy?'

'And didn't you think through any of this before you came to me?' he flared back.

The terrible truth was that she *hadn't* thought through all the repercussions—instead she had been swept along by feelings which had been too primitive to allow any room for reason. She had felt an overpowering sense of injustice—because Constantine might be about to marry another woman and have a family with *her* without realising that he had another son who might know nothing but penury and spend his life living in the shadows. And she had thought he would recognise her—remember the night they had spent together with surely a *bit* of fondness. And then, in true fairy-tale fashion, she had imagined him acknowledging his son with a certain amount of Greek pride.

And it was about you, too, wasn't it? prompted the uncomfortable voice of her conscience. *Aren't you forgetting to put that into the equation? You were unreasonably jealous of the woman you thought was going to share his life—even though you had no right to be. And your actions helped contribute to the fact that the supermodel stormed out of the hotel suite, didn't they?*

'Or did you think I was just going to roll over like a pussycat and sign you a big, fat cheque?' he persisted.

She had been about to admit her hastiness and lack of forethought, but his hateful remark made her bite it back. What an unremittingly cruel man he could be. Perhaps she

had opened a whole can of worms, and Alex might be
about to discover what kind of man his father really was.
'I—I'll organise the test,' she said shakily.

Constantine heard the faint tremble in her voice, and unwillingly he frowned. He remembered the photo of the
little boy with the stubborn curls and the wariness which
had peeped out from his black eyes. Could he really put
the child through the worry of a test? Had she not proved
herself by now? Because surely if she had been bluffing
then she would not have dared sustain such a fiction for so
long. And the fact that he had been trying to block from
his mind now came slamming into focus—that little boy
was *his* little boy.

'Forget the test,' he said suddenly.

Staring out at Milmouth high street, where the hazy
sunshine spilling onto the cobbled streets seemed to mock
at her dark mood, Laura froze. 'F-forget it?' she questioned incredulously. 'Why?'

'I've changed my mind,' he said slowly.

Laura's lips parted—she was scarcely able to believe
what she'd just heard. Constantine magnanimously telling
her that the test was unnecessary when he was the one who
had insisted on it in the first place—like a teacher at school
deciding to let her off a hastily handed-out detention. He
has all the power, she realised bitterly. And she still wasn't
clear what the motives were for his sudden about-face.

'But you said you wanted proof.'

'I no longer need it. I believe you,' he said unexpectedly.

'You believe that he's your son?'

'Yes.' There was a long silence as Constantine acknowledged the power of the single word of admission which
would now change his whole life—whether he liked it or

not. 'Yes, I believe he's my son,' he said heavily, as if the full statement would reinforce that fact to both of them. He had known it the moment he had stared at the photo and seen those disobedient curls—and on some subliminal level he had accepted it even before that. Because some instinct had told him to—an instinct he had not understood at the time and probably never would.

'But…why?' Her confused words cut into the turmoil of his thoughts. 'Why now, after all you said? All you accused me of?'

Constantine curled his hand into a tight fist and stared at it. All he had said had been rooted in denial; he hadn't *wanted* to believe her. He had been reluctant to accept the enormity of the possible consequences if what she said *had* been true. But suddenly he allowed himself to see that this news could have all kinds of benefits—and perhaps it had dropped into his life at just the right time. A solution had begun to form in his mind—as perfect a solution as such circumstances would allow. All he needed was to convince her to go along with it.

The determination which had driven him to rebuild one of the most powerful companies in his native Greece now emerged in a different form. A form which could be used to tackle a private life which had suddenly become complicated. Constantine's mouth hardened, and so did his groin as he remembered the way she had let him kiss her in that scruffy little hotel corridor last night. Of *course* she would go along with his wishes! She wasn't exactly the kind of woman who was going to turn down a golden opportunity if it fell into her lap, now, was she?

For a moment he was tempted to put his proposition to her there and then—until he was reminded that she had shown signs of stubbornness. Better to have her as a captive audience and to tell her face to face. Better to allow his lips and his body to persuade her if his words couldn't.

'Your co-operation has convinced me that you are telling the truth,' he said silkily. 'A woman like you would be unlikely to pit herself against an adversary like me if she was lying.'

The unexpected reprieve made Laura blink her eyes rapidly. 'Th-thank you,' she said, after taking a moment to compose herself—though when she thought about it afterwards she realised that she had completely missed the sting behind his words.

Constantine was aware that this was the moment to choose—when she was both vulnerable and grateful. 'We'll need to discuss some kind of way forward,' he said smoothly. 'Obviously, if I am the child's father, then there are a great many possibilities available to us all in the future.'

Laura felt a conflicting mixture of fear and hope. She didn't like to ask what he meant in case she came over as greedy, or grasping—but her senses had been put on alert. His sudden mood-switch from anger and accusation to honeyed reasonableness was unsettling—she felt like a starving dog, about to leap on a tasty-looking piece of meat, only to discover that it was a mangy old stick. What did he want?

'Such as?' she questioned cautiously.

'I don't really think it's the kind of discussion we should be conducting on the phone do you, *mikros minera*?' His voice deepened. 'So why don't we meet somewhere and talk it over like two sensible adults?'

It didn't seem to matter how many times she swallowed—Laura just couldn't lose the parchment-dryness which seemed to be constricting her throat. Why did she feel as if she was being lured into some trap—as if Constantine Karantinos was taking her down some path to an unknown and not particularly welcome destination? She snatched a glance at her watch. She was already ten minutes over her lunch break, and Sarah would go mad if she was much longer.

'Okay,' she said cautiously. 'I'll meet you. Where and when?'

'As soon as possible,' he clipped out. 'Let's say tomorrow night. I can come there—'

'No!' The word came out in a burst before she steadied her voice. 'Not here. Not yet. People will talk.'

'Why will they talk?' he bit back, more used to his presence at a woman's side being flaunted.

Laura stared out of the window to where she could see the distant glimmer of the sea. Did he have no idea about a small town like this and the ongoing mystery of Alex's paternity? Her night with the handsome Greek had been clandestine enough, and no one had known about it. Previously innocent and still relatively naïve, her pregnancy had come as a complete shock. If Laura's mother had still been alive, it might all have been different—she would have been there to support her and help her face the rest of the world.

As it was, Laura had felt completely on her own—not wanting to burden her young sister with any of her fears about the future. She had been proud and defiant from the moment she'd started to show right up to the moment she'd brought her baby home from the hospital.

Alex had been so very cute, and Laura so tight-lipped about his parentage, that people had given up asking who his father was—even if they still sometimes wondered.

But imagine if a man as commanding and as striking as Constantine should suddenly show up in Milmouth! His black hair and golden-olive skin were exactly the same physical characteristics which marked her son out at school. Why, she might as well take out a front-page advertisement in the *Milmouth Gazette*! People would talk and word might reach Alex—and whatever Alex was going to be told it needed to be carefully thought out beforehand. Oh, *what* was she going to tell her beloved son?

'Because people always talk,' she said flatly. 'And I don't want my son hearing speculative gossip.'

Constantine frowned. 'Where, then? London?'

'London's not easy for me to get to.'

'I can send a car for you.'

How easily practical problems could be solved when you had money, thought Laura. But a Greek billionaire's limousine was just as striking as its owner. 'No, honestly—there's no need for that. I'll meet you in Colinwood—it's our nearest big town.'

Constantine waved away the secretary who had appeared at the door of his vast office, carrying a bundle of papers. 'And is there a good restaurant there?'

She thought about what Colinwood had to offer. 'There's a hotel called the Grapevine, which is supposed to have a good restaurant, but I won't be eating because I like to have tea with my…my son,' she said. And besides, if the evening turned out to be really uncomfortable then she'd be trapped, wouldn't she? Forced to sit enduring food she didn't really want to eat and growing silent every time the waiter appeared. 'I'll meet you in the bar at nine.'

'Very well,' he said softly, and put the phone down—feeling slightly perplexed that she had not instantly fallen in with his wishes as he had expected her to do. *As women always did.*

Laura sat in silence for a moment after the connection was broken, and then ran back down to the empty shop, blurting out her news before her sister had a chance to berate her for being late.

'I'm meeting him for a drink tomorrow night. He's changed his mind about the DNA test.'

Sarah paused in the middle of brushing some icing sugar off the counter. '*Why?*'

Laura shook her head, and a terrible combination of fear and excitement shivered over her skin. 'I *don't know*,' she whispered. 'I just don't know.'

CHAPTER FIVE

DURING the build-up to her meeting with Constantine, Laura tried to carry on as usual—but inside she was still a seething cauldron of nerves, fear, and a terrible sense of *excitement,* too. And how she hated that heart-pounding awareness that she was going to see him again…that she *wanted* to see him again.

Even her choice of clothes for the outing proved a headache—she wasn't used to going out on dates and so had no idea what to wear. And this *wasn't* a date, she reminded herself—in fact, it was anything but. She knew it was wrong to go looking all dressed-up—it might look as if she was *expecting* something, mightn't it? But he had only ever seen her dressed as a waitress—or naked—and she had her pride. She didn't want him to look at her and wonder what the hell he had ever seen in her.

So, the following evening, she tucked Alex into bed and went to shower and change. It was a hot, sticky evening, and a light, flowery dress was about the only thing she had which was suitable—but it worked with bare legs and strappy wedge sandals. She added some seed pearls which had belonged to her mother, and went into the sitting room to face her sister's assessment.

'No make-up?' questioned Sarah critically as she looked her up and down.

'I am wearing a *bit*.'

'Hardly going to knock his socks off looking like that, are you?'

'That was never my intention,' said Laura as she picked up her handbag. 'Anyway, I'll see you later.' She wobbled her sister a smile as nerves came back to assail her. 'And thanks for babysitting.'

'Any time. Ring me if you want rescuing.'

'And how are you going to rescue me?' asked Laura, her mouth curving into a wry smile. 'By sending in the cavalry?'

She caught the bus to Colinwood—a pretty journey, which took in part of the dramatic coastline before tunnelling into lanes lush and thick with summer greenery. Normally she might have enjoyed just sitting back and taking in the scenery, but her heart was full of fear and the sky was heavy with the yellow-grey clouds which preceded a storm. As Laura alighted in the market square in the still and heavy air, she could already feel the oppressive beads of sweat which were prickling at her forehead.

The Grapevine was already quite full—mainly with young professionals, as well as couples out together for the evening. Laura found herself watching them the most—their close body contact proclaiming to the world that they were in love.

She knew that envy was an unappealing trait, but sometimes she just couldn't help herself. She wondered what it must be like to do things the 'right' way round. To fall in love and get engaged and then married. To have a man sit and hold your hand and look as if he had found heaven on earth. She tried to imagine the shared joy of a first baby—

the breathless wonder of news being broken to friends and relatives. Not like her—with her unplanned pregnancy and her young son who had never laid eyes on his father...

She saw Constantine immediately—somehow he had bagged the best table in a quiet corner which commanded an enviable view of the stunning gardens outside. A waitress was buzzing around him, smiling for an extra beat as she placed a small dish of olives in front of him, smoothing her manicured hand down over a slender hip as if she wanted to draw his attention to it.

Please give me the strength to stand up to him, Laura said to herself silently as she picked her way through the room towards him, trying to fix her face into a neutral expression. But what kind of expression did she wear in circumstances like these?

Constantine watched her, observing her with a clinical detachment made easier by the fact that she was not wearing a uniform tonight. Tonight her long, fine hair was fizzing down over her shoulders—he could see its brightness as she approached. And she wore a thin little summer dress which made the most of her firm, young body and slender frame. The shoes she wore were high and drew attention to her legs. Amazing legs, he thought suddenly, as if remembering why she had captivated him all those years ago—and then instantly regretted it as she walked up to his table.

'H-hello, Constantine.'

He should have risen to greet her, but his trousers were stretched so tightly across his groin that he did not dare move. It wasn't textbook behaviour—but then he reminded himself that this wasn't exactly a textbook situation. They weren't out on some kind of cute, getting-to-know-you evening; they were here to discuss a small child. And once again the shimmering of some unknown emotion whispered at his heart.

'Sit down,' he drawled.

'Thanks.' She perched on the edge of the plush leather banquette, her skin clammy and her heart thumping loudly with nerves. It was so hot in here! When he handed her a glass of wine, she automatically took it with boneless fingers, even though she'd decided on the way over that alcohol was a bad idea. She took a sip. 'Have…have you been waiting long?'

There was silence for a moment, and Constantine leaned back, taking his time as he studied her, noting the way her knees were pushed tightly together and the stiff set of her slender shoulders. Her body language screamed out her tension—and he knew then that this was not going to be a walk-over. 'No, I've only just arrived,' he said, and in the fading light his eyes glittered. 'So…that's the niceties out of the way. Have you told the boy anything yet?'

Laura shook her head. She wished he would stop looking at her like that. As if he was stripping her completely bare with his black eyes. 'No.'

Fractionally, he leaned towards her. 'Do you realize,' he said softly, 'that I don't even know his name?'

It sounded like an accusation, and maybe it was—though it was actually the first time he'd asked. She sucked in a breath, disorientated by his proximity. *What if he hates the name I've chosen?* she thought—*in that inexplicable way that people often did take against names because they reminded them of someone or something from their past.*

'It's Alex,' she said quietly. 'Short for Alexander.'

There was a moment of silence before Constantine let

out a long, low breath. It was a name which meant warrior. A proud name which carried with it all the weight and honour of his heritage. 'A Greek name,' he observed.

'Yes. It seemed somehow *appropriate*.'

He felt a wave of something approaching helplessness wash over him. 'In a situation which was entirely *inappropriate*?' he countered—because didn't giving the child a name make him seem real in a way that a photo never could? A person was beginning to emerge from the scraps of information he was being fed. A person about whom he knew absolutely *nothing*. 'What else did you decide was *appropriate*?' he snapped.

Laura recoiled from the anger which was emanating in heated waves from his powerful frame, and she put her wine glass down on the table before it slid from her fingers. 'We can't keep apportioning blame!' she said in a low voice. 'What happened *happened*. We can't change it—we just have to deal with the situation as it is.'

'And the situation is what?' he retorted. 'A woman who is clearly living from hand to mouth having sole charge of my son and heir? Don't you think it's time I had a little input into his life as well, Laura?'

'Of…of course I do. That's why I'm here.' She stared at him, twisting her fingers nervously in her lap. 'We could arrange a first meeting, if you like.'

He gave a short laugh. 'Slot me into the diary like an appointment at the dentist, you mean? You want me turning up on a Saturday afternoon to take a reluctant child for a hamburger while he counts away the minutes he has to spend with this stranger?'

Laura bit her lip. 'I didn't mean like that.'

'No? Then just what *did* you mean?' His black eyes

blazed into her. 'What kind of future had you anticipated when you made contact with me again?'

His dominance was formidable, and Laura felt herself swamped by its dark power. '*I don't know*,' she admitted desperately.

Constantine's mouth hardened. 'Well, I *do*. I have given it a lot of thought and weighed up all the possibilities.' He had spoken to his lawyers, too—but maybe now was not the best time to tell her *that*. He lowered his voice, the way he did in the world of business when he was about to close a deal. 'And there is a future which makes perfect sense for all parties. Which is why I want you to accompany me to my island home in Greece, Laura, occupying the only position which is appropriate.' He paused, and his eyes gleamed like cold, black stones as he looked at her. 'As my wife.'

CHAPTER SIX

LAURA stared at Constantine, her heart beating wildly, scarcely able to believe her ears. 'Your *wife*?' she repeated incredulously. 'Why on earth would I want to marry *you*?'

'*Want* has nothing to do with it,' he iced back, outraged at her shocked and unflattering response. '*Need* is a far more fitting word. For a start, you need money.'

'I never said—'

'You're a *waitress* who also works in a damned shop!' he shot out.

The beating of her heart increased. 'How did you know that?'

His lips twisted. How naïve she was! 'It wasn't difficult. I got someone to find out for me.'

Laura swallowed. 'You mean you've been *spying* on me?'

Dismissively, he batted the question away, with an arrogant flick of his hand. If only it were as easy to bat away the memory of the photos his private detective had dropped in front of him: Laura taking the boy to school in clothes which were clearly too small for him. Not to mention the pictorial evidence of his son growing up in some scruffy apartment over a seedy little shop.

But it was more than that. There had been the dawning

realisation that perhaps this trembling little waitress might actually make ideal marriage material. Poor and desperate—wouldn't she be so swept away by his power and his riches that she would be completely malleable, so that he could mould her to the image of his perfect wife? And of course added to all this was the inexplicable fact that he hadn't been able to stop thinking about that stolen kiss in the dark basement of the hotel... Why, even now the memory of it made him want to do it all over again. It was crazy. It was inexplicable. And it was as potent as hell...

He scowled, forcing his mind back to her ridiculous claim that she'd been spying on him. 'Don't be hysterical, Laura,' he snapped. 'When a woman comes to a man in my position, making claims of enormous significance, it is inevitable her background will be investigated. For all I knew you might have had some male partner at home, his eyes fixed greedily on the main chance—seeing your ex-lover as a meal ticket.'

'You...you...*cynic*...' she breathed.

'Or simply a realist?' he countered. 'Oh, come on—you can lose the outrage, *agape mou*. You see, I *know* the corrupting power of money. And I've seen what people will do in its pursuit.'

Laura stared at him. His *wife*? Had he really just asked her to be his wife? 'But I thought you were marrying that other woman—'

'What other woman?'

She saw his eyes narrow dangerously and wished she hadn't started this. 'The Swedish supermodel,' she said reluctantly.

'Who told you that?'

'I heard it on the radio,' she admitted, and from the look

of slowly dawning comprehension which crossed his face she wished she'd kept quiet. Because now she sounded like some kind of stalker.

'You shouldn't believe a word the media tells you,' he snapped. 'But at least that explains why you suddenly appeared out of nowhere the other night.' His eyes fixed her with icy challenge. 'Actually, the press have been trying to marry me off for years—but *I* will chose whom and when to marry, not the media!'

She stared up at him, full of bewilderment. 'I still don't understand…after everything you've said—why you want to marry *me.*'

'Don't you? Think about it. Marriage has always been on a list as something that perhaps I ought to do when I get around to it—but there's been no real sense of urgency. Until now.' His black eyes glittered. 'You see, I possess a vast fortune, Laura,' he elaborated softly, 'and my father is old and frail. His greatest wish is to see me provide him with an heir. This could be a surprisingly easy way of accomplishing both objectives.'

Laura shook her head. 'But that's so…*cold-blooded*!'

'Is it?' He gave a cynical laugh. 'Unlike you, I have not grown up on a diet of believing in romance and happy-ever-after.' In fact, he knew better than anyone that reality never matched up to dreams, and that emotion robbed men of sense and of reason. He lowered his voice. 'Why not look at it practically rather than emotionally? Marriage will serve a purpose—it will legitimise my son and it will give you all the financial security you could ever need.'

But deep down Laura's suspicions were alerted. It would also give Constantine power, she recognised. And once he had that power wouldn't he be tempted to use it against her? Pushing her to the sidelines until he dominated Alex's life as she suspected that he could all too easily? Everything that she'd fought and worked for could be threatened by this man's undeniable wealth and charisma.

'No! No and no and no!' she flared back, as the emotion and the humid atmosphere of the bar began to tighten her throat. Suddenly she needed to get away from Constantine's heady proximity and the danger he represented.

Grabbing her handbag, she stood up—and without another word walked straight out of the bar, uncaring of the sudden lull in conversation from the couples around them, or the curious eyes watching her as she tried not to stumble in her high wedges.

Outside in the fast-fading light the atmosphere was just as sticky, and the heady scent of roses was almost overpowering. Laura dimly wondered if she should take off her shoes and run to the bus stop in an effort to escape from him, when she felt a hand gripping her arm. Constantine spun her round to face him, his black eyes blazing.

He stared at her, a nerve working furiously in his cheek. Because no woman had ever said no to him before. And no woman ever turned her back on him, either.

'Don't you ever walk out on me like that again!' he bit out.

'I'm a free agent and I can do exactly as I please!'

'You think so?' His mouth hardened with lust. 'Well, in that case, so can I!'

Without warning he pulled her right up against him— so close that she could feel every hard sinew. And she wanted to resist him—just as she was resisting his demand that she marry him. But it seemed that her body had other ideas. To her horror she found herself wanting to sink against him. Into him.

Did he sense that? Was that why he gathered her closer still—with a small moan of what sounded like his own surrender?

In the pale light, he tilted her face up. 'Now, this *is* a time when the word *want* is appropriate. And you want me, Laura—just as I want you. Don't ask me why, but I do,' he ground out, and he drove his mouth down onto hers.

She had meant to gasp out her protest, but instead her lips opened beneath his like a sea-anemone, and suddenly her feelings ran away with her. Was it anger or frustration which fuelled her desire, causing her fingers to clutch at his shoulders—finding the butter-soft silk of his shirt and the hard sheath of the muscular flesh beneath? Or was it something infinitely more dangerous—the fierce clamour of her heart for a man who would never grant her access to his?

'*Oh,*' she breathed, as she felt his free hand move down to splay with intimate freedom over the globe of one buttock, and a shudder rocked through her as her body melted into his.

'*Theos mou*!' he ground back in response. Through waves of hunger, which came with a strength he had not been anticipating, Constantine pulled her into a darkened recess at the side of the building and continued to plunder her mouth with kiss upon kiss. The fingers which had been on her bottom now slipped underneath the little sundress, and he slid his hand round until it lay over the cotton-covered warmth of her mound. He felt her gasp out a little cry. Her passion had not abated over the years, he thought grimly. Nor had her eagerness dulled or softened around the edges. He felt himself grow so hard that he thought he would explode.

Should he do it to her here? Unzip his trousers and thrust himself in her sweet, wild wetness? He moved his hand over what felt like a pair of functional cotton panties.

'If only you weren't wearing any…then how easy it would be,' he commented unevenly.

His graphic words broke into the darkly erotic spell which had captivated her, and Laura opened her eyes to see the face of Constantine—taut and tight with sexual hunger. Reality washed over her like a cold shower. *What the hell was she doing? Standing there while he put his hand between her legs and incited her to…to…*

'Stop…stop it,' she whispered.

'Stop what?'

'T-touching me.'

'But you like it. You know you do.' He moved a finger against her and heard her breathing quicken. 'Don't you?'

'*Oh.*'

His fingertips continued to tease her moist heat—and even in the dim light he could see the sudden dilation of her eyes before the lids came down to obscure them. She relaxed against him once more and he felt her imminent surrender. Should he carry on? Bring her to an orgasm she would be unable and unwilling to prevent? Kiss away the gasping little sounds as those sweet spasms pulsed through her? It would be a turn-on to watch her, and perhaps she would be more amenable to his plans if he had her glowing and basking in his arms afterwards.

But at that moment he heard the sound of a car approaching, and saw the powerful beam of its headlights snaking up the drive. He realised just what he was doing. He, Constantine Karantinos, was standing by the side of a hotel, making out with a woman, in an aroused state such as he had not been in since his teenage youth!

'Let's go upstairs,' he murmured, his lips soft as they whispered over the long pale line of her neck.

Through the mists of sweet, sensual hunger warning bells sounded like fire alarms in her head, and Laura opened her eyes in confusion. 'Up-upstairs?' she echoed blankly.

'Mmm. Much more comfortable there. Enormous bed. Enormous pleasure.' He kissed her neck and guided her fingers to where he was hard and aching for her. 'Enormous everywhere,' he whispered, on an arrogant boast.

But Laura shrank back, snatching her hand away from his tantalising heat as she looked up at him, aghast. 'You have a *room* here?'

'A suite, actually. Not the best I've seen—but not bad.'

'Let me get this straight.' Her heart was pounding. 'You thought...you thought that I'd just meekly go to bed with you?'

He smiled. 'Meekly is not the word I was hoping for, *agape mou*—since your response so far tells me that you are a very passionate woman. But then as I recall you always were,' he added softly.

And it was those last words of his which were almost her undoing—because they gave the situation a *faux* intimacy, almost as if they had some kind of tender, shared past between them. But they didn't, she reminded herself painfully. What they had shared had been nothing but a powerful sexual chemistry which had flared out of control. And just because that sexual chemistry was as explosive as ever, it didn't mean she had to give in to it. To behave in a way which would afterwards have him insulting her as if she were no better than a cheap little tramp.

'I'm not going upstairs with you,' she said sharply, pulling herself out of his arms and tugging her dress down defiantly as she moved away from the alcove.

To Constantine's astonishment, he could see that she

meant it. Had he thought that she would capitulate as easily as she had done all those years ago? The way women always did? For a moment frustrated longing pulsed around his veins as he searched her face for a sign that she might be on the verge of changing her mind, but there was none.

With the steely self-control for which he was renowned he forced his own desire to evaporate, like droplets of water sizzling onto a hot Greek street. There would be plenty of time for sex once she had agreed to his other demands—and, banishing the tantalising memory of her heated response to him, Constantine switched to the real reason he was here.

'Hasn't that little interlude convinced you that we could make a creditable stab at matrimony?' he questioned softly as he followed her, his feet crunching over the soft gravel.

'How delightfully you put it—but the answer is still no.' Her knees still weak, Laura sank down onto a wooden bench in full view of the main entrance into the hotel, where cars were coming and going. Let him *dare* try to start touching her here!

Constantine sat down next to her. Was this like a board-room battle? he wondered. With her supposedly stubborn resistance being used as a lever to increase her demands? He gave a small smile. She would soon learn that *he* called all the shots. 'I'd like to know what your main objection to my proposal is?' he questioned silkily.

'Why—Alex, of course,' she shot back. 'Do you really think I can just announce to him that I'm marrying his father—whom he's never even met—and that we're all going off to Greece to live happily ever after?'

'Why not?'

'Why *not*? Don't you know *anything* about children?'

'Actually, no, I don't,' he snapped. 'Since I've been denied that opportunity up until now!'

Laura swallowed as she stared into the shadowed flint of his features. Be reasonable, she told herself as she worked out what to say. Because if she expected him to come round to her way of thinking then she was going to have to be convincing. And convincing a man like this about anything wasn't going to be easy. She had to show him how it would look from a little boy's point of view.

Her voice softened. 'Alex's life is here in England— it's all he's ever known. Don't you think that suddenly landing all this in his lap would be overloading him with too much, too soon? Tearing him away from his home and his school? A new father who turns up out of the blue and a new life he has no say in? What if Greece doesn't work out?'

'We will make it work out,' he vowed grimly.

And in a way that stubborn insistence only reinforced her determination. Laura suddenly got an ominous vision of the finality of being trapped in a loveless marriage with a man like Constantine, and a shiver ran down her spine. 'You can't *make* things happen like that,' she said. 'Human beings aren't puppets that you can play with and control. I don't think you realise the impact of taking a child who's never even been abroad and plonking him in a foreign land.'

His body tensed as if she had hit him, and he clenched his fists. 'Don't ever...*ever*...refer to Greece as a "foreign land" in front of me or in front of my son,' he hissed. 'It is the land of his forebears with a rich and glorious heritage. And one which I intend that he will learn about.'

The fingers which had tightened into two fists now

slowly unfurled, and Laura found herself watching them with a horrible kind of fascination.

'I want contact with Alex,' he continued inexorably. 'And I want him to meet his grandfather. Those two things are non-negotiable—so how do you intend to let me go about doing it, Laura?'

And Laura knew then that she didn't have to be stuck on an island to be trapped. Entrapment could be emotional as well as geographical, she realised—and in a way her fate had been sealed from the moment she had made contact with him again. She could see the determination etched on his face, and she realised that there was no way she was going to be able to escape his demands. Which meant that she had to fashion them to best suit her and Alex's purpose. And no one could deny that it was in a child's best interests to learn about his father—no matter what *she* thought about him.

She laced her fingers together. 'I think it's best for Alex to get to know you…gradually.'

'And how do you suggest I do that?' he demanded. 'Start coming into that bread shop you run and buying some damned bun every morning?'

If the circumstances hadn't been so fraught then Laura might almost have laughed, because the image of this powerful Greek going into her little village shop was both bizarre and amusing. But there was no place for humour here; this was deadly serious. Yet neither was there was any need for him to be so scathing about her method of earning a living. Working in a shop wasn't up there with being a supermodel, but it was honest and it was decent—even if it didn't reap the huge kind of rewards which *he* obviously considered essential.

'Of course I don't,' she said stiffly.

'*My* life and *my* work are in Greece,' he clipped out.

'I realise that.' Just as hers and Alex's was here—a cultural and geographical world away. Laura's mind starting spinning as she searched desperately for some sort of solution to their dilemma, when suddenly a thought occurred to her. Unseen in the folds of her cheap summer dress, her fingers tightened as an idea of breathtaking simplicity came to her. 'But the long summer holidays are coming up,' she said slowly.

Constantine stilled. 'And what has that got to do with anything?'

'I could come to Greece,' she said carefully. 'But not as your wife. A complete lifestyle change would unsettle Alex—but he could cope with the kind of situation he's used to.'

'You aren't making any sense,' he snapped.

'Well, I...I presume that your father employs staff at his home in Greece?'

'Of course he does.'

'How many?'

'I am not in the habit of keeping an inventory,' he drawled. But her eyes continued to regard him steadily and he gave an impatient kind of sigh. 'There is a permanent housekeeper who lives within the complex, and several people who come in from the village to help out.'

'And do...do any of them have children?'

'Not young children, no—but there are plenty of those in the village.' He frowned. 'What the hell does that have to do with anything?'

Laura let out a long breath. 'I know exactly what we can do,' she breathed. 'You take me on for the summer as a temporary member of staff. I can work in your father's house—'

'*Work in my father's house*?' he roared in disbelief, staring at her as if she had taken complete leave of her senses. 'Doing *what*?'

Laura lifted her chin up, determined not to be intimidated by the fierce blaze from his eyes. 'The skills of which you've already been so very critical—I can clean and make beds. I can serve food. I can even cook—though not to any cordon bleu standard.'

Constantine stared into her face. 'Such lowly and subservient pursuits!' he bit out. 'What kind of a woman would want this?'

A woman with pride, thought Laura ardently. And a woman with dignity—or rather one who was trying to claw back some of the poise which always seemed to fly out of the window whenever Constantine was around.

'Meanwhile, Alex gets a few weeks in the sun,' she carried on, her enthusiasm growing now. 'If he plays with other children he can learn a little Greek, and they can learn English. It'll do him good to have a holiday—and in that relaxed environment he can get to know you.'

There was an ominous kind of silence while Constantine mulled over her words—there was no doubt that he was surprised by the humbleness of her request. She wanted to come to his house as a *servant*! And yet maybe it would work out better this way—for wouldn't it place strain on his father's heart to suddenly produce a seven-year-old grandson out of nowhere? And wouldn't she be more expendable as a servant than as a wife? Easier to dispose of afterwards, if her presence began to grate on him, without having to go through all the publicity and disruption of a divorce?

He stared at her, aware that her impudent idea was distracting him from the most important question of all. 'And when do you propose telling Alex that I'm his father?' he asked softly.

The eyes she turned to him were huge. 'Can we...can we wait until the moment is right?'

He hardened his heart against the tremulous appeal in her voice. 'I will not wait for ever, Laura,' he warned.

'No. No, I can understand that. We will tell him as soon as it's appropriate. I promise. Oh, thank you. Thank you, Constantine.' She flashed him a grateful smile, but the look he gave in response was like ice.

'This is not a situation I am happy with,' he bit out.

How hard the years had made him, she thought fleetingly. He was a completely different person from the ruffle-haired man who had sailed in and out of her life all those summers ago.

And what about her? Had *she* changed that much? Laura bit her lip. Quite honestly, that brief period of freedom and sexual awakening had been so unlike anything she had known since that she had almost completely forgotten it. Or maybe she had just blocked it from her mind. Maybe it was too painful to remember being carefree and unencumbered by worry.

She forced her mind back to practicalities. 'The only problem I can think of is that I'm going to need a replacement to help my sister in the shop while I'm away—but I assume you'd be able to help me sort that out?'

The *only* problem? he thought. Was she crazy? He could see a few more than that.

'I can fix that,' said Constantine heavily—because for the first time in his life he had not got what he wanted. Despite her reduced circumstances and tiny stature, he could see that here was a woman who had her mind set on something, and nothing he could do or say was going to change her mind. Was this a unique version of mother-love? he wondered bitterly. A mother fighting tooth and nail for what was best for her child?

Briefly, Constantine found himself wondering what it must be like to have a mother who felt like that about you. A mother who cared about your welfare more than she cared about her own—but he vetoed the thought instantly. He never wasted time thinking about things which were beyond his own comprehension.

It was one of the reasons behind his success.

CHAPTER SEVEN

LAURA was aware of a surprisingly green oval rising up to meet them as the helicopter landed with the agility of a large moth. Ringed with silver-white sand, from the sky the island had looked like a jewel in the middle of a sea so intensely blue that she'd felt quite shaken with the beauty of it all.

And shaken by her first ever trip in a helicopter, of course.

She stole a glance at Alex, who also seemed completely rapt by the splendour unfolding before him, and wondered what kind of effect this trip was going to have on him. Because although she'd insisted on travelling out to Greece on a regular airline, since 'servants don't arrive in private jets,' as she had told Constantine firmly, there had been a helicopter waiting at Athens airport to whisk them off to the island of Livinos.

It had all proved a little distracting—and Laura found herself wondering if experiencing these enormous riches from such an early age had been instrumental in fashioning Constantine's character? She stared out at the gradually slowing helicopter blades. Of course it had! Your early experiences always shaped your development like nothing else. If he'd been used to snapping his fingers from an early age and getting whatever it was he wanted then no wonder he was so autocratic and demanding.

She held Alex's hand tightly as she helped him down from the helicopter, with his beloved blue bear clutched tightly to his chest. He'd been worried that the scruffy old toy was too babyish to bring with him—but Laura had insisted the bear come too. Heaven only knew he wouldn't go to sleep without him.

Thinking she heard someone call her name, she looked up, her eyes narrowed against the blinding heat of the hot sun, and there, standing beside a four-wheel drive, was the man who had been dominating her thoughts all week.

Constantine! Here! Her mouth dried and her heart began to race erratically as he fixed his piercing gaze on them. So much hung on what happened next, and for Alex's sake she prayed that this first meeting would be a success as they made their way across the scorching tarmac towards the Greek billionaire.

Constantine felt a sudden lurching of his heart as he watched them approach, unprepared for the powerful feelings which came surging over him as he stared at the boy. The photos he had seen had made him take seriously her claim that the child was his—even though he had done his best to deny it at the time. But seeing him now, in the living and breathing flesh—well, that was something entirely different. Put a hundred—no, a thousand seven-year-old boys in front of him and Constantine would have instantly picked out this particular boy as having sprung from Karantinos loins.

He sucked in a ragged breath as they grew closer, his heart now pounding with a terrible combination of recognition and regret—that they were strangers to one another, and yet he knew that they were linked in the most primeval way of all.

With an effort he tore his gaze away from Alex and let it travel instead to Laura, whose eyes were fixed on him with a certain amount of trepidation. As well they might be. Constantine's lips curved with contempt. Another cheap little dress and a pair of sandals which had seen better days—and her fine hair all mussed up in a cloud around her head. Had she deliberately come here today emphasising her lowly status, after stubbornly insisting that she be employed in the house as a member of staff? Was she perhaps hoping that he might make some kind of generous settlement on her if she insisted on highlighting the differences between them?

Yet despite the anger he felt towards her there was a fair amount of it directed at himself, for the inexplicable lust he still felt for her. That his groin should instantly ache with an unquenchable desire to make love to her—this pale and insipid little shop-worker who had turned down his offer of marriage!

But he composed his face into a smile of welcome as they grew closer—because he was clever enough to know that he could never win the boy if he was seen to be openly critical of his mother.

'C-Constantine,' stumbled Laura. 'I…well, I certainly wasn't expecting to find you here to meet us.'

'What an unexpected pleasure it must be,' he murmured sardonically, but his eyes were fixed on the child and he was aware of a strange beating of his heart. 'Hello, Alex.'

Alex turned a confused face up towards Laura 'Who's this, Mum?'

Constantine crouched down so that he was on a level

with the boy, wondering if there would be some kind of instant recognition on the part of his son—but of course there was none. Had he perhaps been secretly hoping that Laura might already have told him—that there would be some kind of touching scene outside the airport? But things like that only happened in movies, he told himself grimly. This was real life.

Usually he did not care what kind of impression he made—people could either take him or leave him. His careless attitude stemmed from the fact that other men were always anxious to be his friend, while women were eager to be his lover. But now he realised that unexpectedly his heart was beating fast with something approaching concern. I want him to like me, he thought fiercely. I *need* him to like me.

'My name is Constantine Karantinos,' he said softly. 'And you are going to be staying in my father's house.'

Alex nodded, as if this were nothing untoward, and Laura supposed that after the excitement of the day itself he would have calmly accepted being told he was taking a trip to the moon. 'Is it a nice house?'

'Oh, it's a very nice house,' answered Constantine, with a smile of rare indulgence. 'With a big swimming pool.'

Alex blinked. 'You mean, just for us?'

'Just for us,' replied Constantine gravely.

Alex bit his lip in the way he always did when he was worried, and Laura's heart turned over as she watched him. 'But I'm not very good at swimming,' he said.

Constantine wondered why. 'Then we shall have to teach you—would you like that?'

Alex nodded, his dark eyes wide. 'Yes, please!'

'Let's get in the car, then.' And Constantine helped the

child into the back seat and strapped him in, before stepping back to allow Laura to pass.

His eyes narrowed as she moved close enough for him to be able to get the drift of some light scent, and despite its cheapness he swallowed with another unexpected wave of lust.

'You look…' He allowed his gaze to drift over her pale skin and pinched expression and saw her bite her lip in response to his critical scrutiny. 'Pretty tired,' he conceded.

'Yes,' said Laura, thinking that tired didn't even come close—she felt physically and mentally exhausted. Truth to tell, she hadn't had a full night's sleep since she'd met Constantine at the Grapevine that night—plus she'd been working some of Sarah's shifts, to make up for the time she was going to take off. 'It's been a long week,' she said wearily.

For a moment—just for a moment—he felt the faintest tug of sympathy. For the first time he noticed that the grey eyes were shadowed, and that her pale skin was almost translucent with fatigue.

'Then for heaven's sake get in the car and relax,' he said roughly, climbing into the driver's seat himself and starting up the engine, while the helicopter pilot put their small and rather battered suitcases in the boot.

'Wow! Get in, Mum!' Alex enthused. 'It's huge.'

Uncomfortably conscious of trying to keep as much of her pale, bare legs hidden as possible, Laura got in next to her son. She caught sight of a pair of black eyes mocking her as they glanced at her from the rearview mirror, and her reaction to that unmistakably sensual look was instinctive, though completely unwelcome. She felt the weak, thready patter of her heart and the icing of her skin, but she stared straight ahead at his broad shoulders and prayed that he would just let her get on with her work while he got down to the important business of getting to know Alex. Did he realise that she was determined to fight her desire for him—since no good could come out of their renewing a sexual relationship?

'Do you live near the sea?' piped up Alex.

'No place on the island is far from it,' answered Constantine. 'And if you're very lucky you might see one of the Karantinos ships sailing by.'

Alex failed to keep the sense of wonder from his voice. 'You mean *real* ships?'

Constantine laughed. 'Yes. Very real. And very big.'

'I'd love that,' said Alex wistfully, and then bit his lip in the way he'd unconsciously picked up from his mother. 'But Mum will be working, won't she? And she says I'm not to get in anyone's way.'

There was an awful silence, and if there had been a dark corner nearby then Laura would have gone away and crawled into it. She had never felt sorry for herself—ever. She had always embraced hard work and considered it a part and parcel of bringing up a child out of wedlock. But Alex's words prompted a deep dislike of her predicament—and of what it was doing to her son.

His words had set them apart. Making him sound like some servant's child from a different century—almost as if he was going to be sent up the chimney and asked to sweep it! And Constantine clearly felt it, too—because once more he caught her gaze in the driving mirror, but this time the look was not remotely sensual, it was spitting with a slow, burning anger. As if it was an insult to *his* honour to hear his son speaking in such a way.

'You must not worry about your mother's working

hours,' he said abruptly. 'Since I know that she will be happy for you to enjoy yourself.'

'I just don't want her to feel left out,' said Alex loyally, and Laura could have wept. It was supposed to be *her* protecting him, and not the other way round.

'Of course you must let Constantine show you all his ships,' said Laura, as if she discussed the ownership of ships every day of her life.

'I used to live here when I was about your age,' said Constantine conversationally.

'Oh, *wow*!' Alex sighed. 'Lucky you.'

Something in the boy's wistfulness made a rush of unwilling memories come flooding back—and for once Constantine could not block them out. In many ways it had been a textbook and idyllic upbringing—with none of the stresses surrounding life spent in the city. The beauty of Livinos, and the ability to swim and to fish and to climb trees without fear—those were gifts which every other child on the island had experienced. He hadn't needed to be the son of a wealthy man to enjoy the carefree freedoms of childhood in this part of Greece.

But, essentially, it had been a lonely time for Constantine. Materially rich but emotionally neglected by a mother who had never been there—even when she had been physically present. His beautiful, fragile mother, who had captivated his father like a moth to a flame—who had consumed all those around her but given little back. Who had not known—nor been able to learn—how to love the strong-minded baby she had given birth to.

'Look out of the window, Alex,' said Constantine gently. 'As well as some of the most wonderful beaches you will ever see, we have mountains, and forests of cedar, oak and pine. And mines of silver and gold.'

'*Gold*?' spluttered Alex. 'Not really?'

'Yes, really. It was first discovered by the Parians, who came from the island of Paros.'

This time Laura sent Constantine a silent message. *Stop it,* her eyes appealed. *Stop painting for him the kind of pictures he has only ever seen in films or books before. Please don't make his life in England fade into pale and boring insignificance.*

And Constantine read the appeal perfectly, deliberately choosing to ignore it. Did she really expect him to play his heritage down, when it was his son's heritage, too? His expression didn't alter.

'We have white marble, too,' he continued. 'Which is exported all over the world. And there are all the other components which are an essential part of Greek life—fruit and honey and olives. Now, look closely as we drive up this road, Alex, and you will see my father's house.'

House, he had said, noted Laura suddenly, her quibble forgotten as she gazed curiously out of the window. Not home. Did that have any significance? But then she peered out through the window and her breath caught in her throat as the most beautiful place she had ever seen suddenly came into view.

Surrounded by orange and lemon trees, the villa was large and imposing, dominating the landscape while somehow managing to blend into it. It stood almost at the top of the mountain, and the views around it were panoramic. Dark sapphire brush-strokes of a sea threw off a brilliant light, and as Laura opened the car door she could smell the scent of pine and citrus and hear the unfamiliar sound of beautiful birdsong.

'We're here,' said Constantine, as he held his hand out to help Alex down. The boy took it as naturally as breathing.

How easily Alex is learning to trust him, thought Laura—knowing that she should be glad for her son's sake, and yet unable to prevent the strange spike of envy which tugged at her stomach.

The huge front door opened and a middle-aged woman wearing a floral pinafore dress came out immediately to meet them—as if she had been standing waiting for their arrival.

'I'll introduce you to Demetra,' Constantine said, an odd glint in his eyes. 'She's in charge of the staff here— so you'll be directly answerable to her. Oh, and don't worry—she speaks excellent English, so you won't have any problems understanding her instructions, Laura.'

Instructions. Answerable. His words brought Laura tumbling back down to earth with a crash. And with a shock she realised that all the privileges she had been enjoying up until that moment were now about to evaporate. She was to become one of the domestic staff. *But that's what you wanted*, she reminded herself painfully. *That's what you insisted on.*

At least she had spent the last few evenings poring over a phrasebook—but her usual slowness with reading coupled with the difficulty of the complex Greek language meant that she had retained only a few words. Still, now was the time to start using them.

'*Kalimera*,' she said, with a nervous smile at the older woman.

Demetra's eyes swept over Laura in rapid assessment, and she said something in Greek to Constantine, to which he made a drawled reply. It seemed to satisfy her, for she nodded and returned the smile.

'*Kalimera*, Laura. You are very welcome at Villa Thavmassios.' Her eyes crinkled fondly as she stared at Alex's dark curls. 'And this your boy?'

'Yes, this is Alex.' Laura gave a Alex a little push, and to her relief he stepped forward and shook the Greek woman's hand, just the way she'd taught him to. Demetra gave a delighted exclamation before enfolding him in a bear-hug, and Laura bit back a smile as she saw Alex send her a horrified look of appeal.

'We bring children from the village to play with you, Alex,' said Demetra. 'And my own son is home from university—he is a very fine sports student. He teach you to swim and to fish. You would like that?'

'Yes, please,' said Alex shyly, as Demetra finally let him go. She said something else to Constantine, but he shook his head.

'*Ochi*,' he said in negation, and then smiled. 'Shall I show you to your room now, Alex?' Then he turned to Laura, almost as if it was an afterthought. 'And I might as well show you yours,' he added softly.

Laura tried to tell herself not to react to the unmistakable provocation in those dark eyes—telling herself that nothing was going to happen because she didn't want anything to happen. But even as she made the silent vow she had to fight to suppress the glimmer of longing which had begun to whisper its way over her skin.

Liar. You know that you want him. That you would give a king's ransom for his lips to rove all over your naked body.

Laura's cheeks flushed, and she could feel their colour intensify simply because Constantine was looking at her with that hateful half-smile playing around his lips—as if he knew exactly what she was thinking. As if he knew that her breasts were prickling and her heart racing like a piston. Her fist clenched around the strap of her handbag and she dug her nails into it—as if she were digging them into his rich, silken flesh.

What on earth was going on? Why was she suddenly reacting to him as if she was the kind of woman who was prey to carnal desires, when nothing could be further from the truth?

Nothing.

Why, there hadn't been a single man in her life since Constantine had sailed away all those years ago—because the truth was that she had never wanted another man in the way she'd wanted him, even if single motherhood didn't exactly encourage romantic entanglements. But suddenly Laura's lack of another lover seemed more like a failure rather than anything to be proud of. As if she was one of those pathetic women who had been carrying a flame for a man who'd never even given her a second thought. Who hadn't even remembered that they'd been lovers!

His voice cut across her thoughts. 'Ready?' he questioned.

Forcing a smile, she took Alex's hand. 'Let's go and see your room, darling.'

The villa was cool and huge—it made her Milmouth apartment look like a shoebox—and Laura found herself wondering how long it would take to get her bearings.

Alex's suitcase had already been brought into a bright room which had been transformed into a small boy's dream. There was a bookcase filled with any number of books, and a table on which sat a drawing block and a rainbow collection of colouring pens. A giant castle reposed in one corner—with small figures of knights and horses—and a beautiful wooden train-set sat curved and just itching to be put in motion.

Seeing the castle, Alex turned to Constantine with a look of breathless excitement on his face.

'Did Mum tell you I liked horses?' he demanded excitedly.

'I thought that all little boys liked horses,' answered Constantine solemnly.

'Can I play with it? Now?'

'That is what it is there for. You play with it while I show your mama her room—which is just along the corridor—then we will go downstairs and eat something, and later on you can swim. Would you like that?'

Alex's eyes were like dark, delighted saucers. 'Oh, *yes*!' And he ran over to the castle.

Laura looked up at Constantine, fighting to keep her emotions in check—but, whichever way you looked at it, the Greek tycoon had gone out of his way to make the small boy feel welcome, and she found that she was having to blink back sudden tears. She wanted to say thank you, but the look which had darkened his features into a steely mask was not one which readily invited gratitude.

'Let's go,' said Constantine softly, and Laura's heart was pounding heavily as they walked along the cool, marbled corridor. She felt like a prisoner whose fate had been sealed, yet she was filled with a terrible kind of excitement when Constantine halted before a door. As he threw it open, all she could see was a bed.

'What did Demetra say to you outside?' she questioned quickly, wanting something—anything—to distract her attention from that bed.

'That you looked too small and too slight for any kind of physical work.'

'And what did you tell her?'

Constantine paused as he stared down into the stormy beauty of her grey eyes, registering the dormant strength which lay within her petite frame. 'I told her that you were no stranger to hard work,' he said unexpectedly.

'Oh.' The words caught her off-guard, and Laura found herself feeling ridiculously warmed by the nearest thing to a compliment he'd paid her. She looked up at him, heart racing. 'Why, thank you—' But she got no further, because Constantine's gaze was raking over her face. He took her hand, pulling her inside the bedroom, shutting the door on the rest of the world.

'Be very clear about this, Laura. I don't want your thanks,' he said softly. 'I want you. *This...*' And suddenly he was kissing her with a fervour which sapped the last of her resistance. Her knees sagged and she fell against him as with a low moan he tightened his arms around her, his lips prising hers open with effortless mastery.

It was a frantic, seeking kiss, and for a few seconds Laura gave herself up to it completely. She felt the lick of his tongue exploring hers, the sweet pressure of his mouth as it seemed to plunder deeper and deeper within her mouth—until she felt as if he had stripped her bare with his kiss. Suddenly she was vulnerable. Too vulnerable.

She could feel her breasts begin to prickle as they pushed against the hard wall of his chest, and an unbearable aching clamoured at the fork of her thighs. She wanted him to lift her skirt up. She wanted him to touch her. She wanted...

Had she silently transmitted those wishes to Constantine? Because suddenly he was making them all come true. His hand was impatiently rucking up the cotton of her sundress and splaying with indolent possession over the cool silk of her inner thigh.

'Constantine,' she moaned into his mouth, and the sound seemed to incite him.

'Ah, *ne, ne,*' he breathed, as he deepened the kiss, moving his fingertips upwards so that they scorched their way over the moist fabric of her panties and he felt her buck beneath him. Would there be time? he wondered distractedly as his hand moved down to his belt.

Through the hot heat of a fierce sexual hunger which seemed ready to consume her Laura felt the sudden tension in his body, and became graphically aware of his growing hardness. And with a certainty born of instinct rather than experience she saw just where all this was leading. Was that the rasping of a zip she could hear? With a stifled cry of horror and recrimination she tore her lips away and pushed helplessly at the solid wall of his chest, but her head dipped against it for support.

'We...we mustn't,' she breathed against his racing heart. 'You know we mustn't.'

Constantine caught his breath before disengaging himself, propelling her away from him as if she had suddenly become poison in his arms. He turned away to adjust his trousers even as hot, sexual hunger coursed round his veins, and it was a moment or two until he had composed himself enough to face her.

And in a way he knew she was right to stop things before they went too far, but—damn her—he didn't *want* her to be right! Especially when she was so turned on and struggling to control her breath. *He* was the one who always controlled the situation, and women the ones who clung to him like limpets as they waited for his command.

The whole encounter had lasted only a couple of minutes but fierce frustration made him turn on her.

'Do you always conduct yourself in such a way?' he accused hotly. 'Using your eyes to beg silently for a man to *take you* when your son is just along the corridor? How many times has he witnessed his mother in an intimate embrace with a man, Laura—tell me that? How many?'

Laura's mouth opened in an 'oh' of protest. 'Never,' she breathed fiercely, shaking her head so that her hair flew round it like a cloud. 'Never, ever.'

'A woman who turns on as quickly as you do? I don't believe you,' he said with soft scorn.

'Don't you? Well, that's your problem, not mine, Constantine—you can believe what you damned well like!' Injustice bubbled up in her blood to replace the aching fires of frustration. Why should he apportion blame solely to *her*? Smoothing her hands down over her heated cheeks, she stared at him. 'You had nothing to do with what just happened, of course—you were just standing there like an innocent while I threw myself at you.'

'I wouldn't advise that you go down the accusation path,' he drawled arrogantly. 'Because when a woman has sent out the unmistakable message that she wants a man to make love to her then I'm afraid that nature has programmed that man to follow through.'

Laura stilled as she stared at him in horror. *Had* she? Her heart began to pound anxiously. Maybe she had—though certainly not consciously—and yet wasn't his reaction to it about as insulting as it was possible to get? As if kissing her had been nothing more than a conditioned response for him, while for her it had been...

What? Her betraying body shivered with sweet memory.

What had it been? Like being transported straight to paradise without stopping? Or—even worse—a reactivation of that passionate longing he had awoken in her the very first time she'd looked into his eyes all those years ago? When she'd believed in love at first sight and had cried for months after he'd gone.

But such emotion was completely wasted. *He doesn't like you*, she reminded herself bitterly—*and he certainly doesn't respect you*. For him you're just another willing body in a long line of willing bodies who have been welcoming him into their arms all his life.

Once she had been blinded by youth and inexperience and his sheer charisma, and she had willingly fallen into bed with him. But now things were different. She had too much to lose to risk throwing it all away on some feel-good sex which would leave her physically satisfied but emotionally bereft. Sex which he might use against her to paint a black picture of her morals. Or which might prejudice her attempts to have a reasonable relationship with him for the sake of his son.

'Shall we just put it down to experience and make sure it doesn't happen again?' she questioned unsteadily.

Black eyes mocked her. 'You think it's that easy? That desire is like a tap you can just turn on and off at will?'

'I think you can try.'

'But I don't want to try,' he said softly. 'And what is more I don't intend to.'

Their eyes met in a silent battle of wills, and Laura felt her mouth dry, hating the fact that his thinly veiled threat thrilled her instead of shocking her. 'I think that…that you'd better leave now while I freshen up and then help get Alex properly unpacked,' she said. But she couldn't help noticing the pulse which beat so frantically at his throat as his gaze continued to rake over her in a look of unashamed sexual hunger.

Laura swallowed as she turned away and walked over to the window, blind to the beauty of the sapphire sea and cerulean sky outside, suddenly realising how difficult this whole situation was going to be. But you're here as his *employee*, she reminded herself. So why not remind him of that? Put some space and some barriers between the two of you. Remind yourself that you are most certainly not equals.

She turned round and fixed the kind of smile to her lips which she gave to the Milmouth office workers when they came into the shop for their lunchtime sandwich. 'So... what happens next in terms of me starting work?'

Constantine gave a slow smile. He knew exactly what she was doing—but he recognised that it was a kind of game she was playing. So let her be confronted by the reality of waiting on him and see how she liked *that!* 'Tonight you and Alex will eat with Demetra, and she will familiarise you with our customs. She will tell you what she expects from you and answer any questions you might have,'

'You mean...you...won't be there?' questioned Laura tentatively.

'No, *agape mou*,' he said softly. 'I'm going out.'

'Out?' she echoed, aware that she sounded crestfallen. And *possessive*?

'Indeed I am.' His black eyes glittered. 'As your new husband I should not, of course, have dreamt of abandoning you on your first evening. But this was the choice you made, Laura—and you must live with the consequences even if they are not to your liking.'

'At least I can live with my conscience,' she said tightly.

'Well, bravo for you!' he mocked, as he finished tucking in his silk shirt. 'And tomorrow Alex will join me and my father for lunch. The child will meet his grandfather for the first time.'

'That's good.' Laura stared at him, suddenly aware of just how little she really knew about him. 'And...your mother?'

There was an infinitesimal pause before he spoke. 'My mother died many years ago,' he said.

'Oh, I'm sorry,' said Laura, interpreting his flat tone as grief, knowing from her own experience that the dead must always be acknowledged, even if the subject sometimes made you feel miserable. 'What happened?' she questioned gently.

'She died of pneumonia a long time ago,' he said, his face stony. 'But my family history need not concern you, Laura.'

'It's Alex's family history, too,' she reminded him, taken aback by the sudden venom in his tone.

'Then I will discuss such matters with Alex,' he said. 'And it's pointless looking at me with those wounded grey eyes—because as my wife you could have legitimately shared such discussions. As it is there are plenty of other things to occupy you. So why don't you run along and speak to Demetra.'

He paused deliberately, enjoying seeing the flush of colour to her cheeks, wanting to rub in the subservience she had insisted on. Wanting to wound her as she had somehow wounded him, though he couldn't for the life of him work out how. 'And then prepare to wait on my table,' he finished cuttingly.

CHAPTER EIGHT

LAURA awoke to that confusing sensation of being in a strange room and not realising quite where she was—until she saw the stripes of bright sunlight shafting in through the bottom of the shutters and felt unaccustomed warm air wafting her body. She was in Greece—on the Karantinos island—and all night long she'd dreamt of Constantine, remembering the coldness in his voice when she'd tried to ask him about his mother, his dismissing her and her questions with a crisp arrogance clearly intended to drive home her reduced status in his household.

Some time during the night she must have kicked off the crisp cotton sheet, and now she was lying sprawled and exposed in a little nightdress which had ridden up over her hips during her very restless sleep. Which was surprising, given how tired she'd been following a delicious supper eaten with Demetra and her son in the cosy informality of the large kitchen.

Afterwards she and Alex had gone for a walk around the vast estate, with Demetra's son, Stavros, acting as their guide. The young Greek student had pointed out all the bright constellations in the night sky and Alex had had the time of his life as a brand-new world of astronomy had opened up for him.

And then Laura sat bolt upright in bed. Alex! She hadn't heard a peep out of him all night—when she'd tucked him and Blue Bear up in bed he'd barely been able to murmur goodnight before he was out for the count. What if he'd had nightmares? Got up and gone looking for her? Or wanted a drink and found himself lost in this vast and unknown house?

Grabbing her matching wrap, she hurried from her room and burst into Alex's room—to find it completely empty. 'Alex!' she gasped.

'He's outside,' came a voice from behind her, and she whirled around to find Constantine standing in the doorway of the room—an unfathomable look on his face as he studied her.

Aware that her hair was unbrushed and her eyes still full of sleep, Laura blinked. 'Outside where?'

'By the pool—with Demetra's son.'

'You mean you left my son—'

'*Our* son,' he corrected.

'With someone who's virtually a stranger—by a swimming pool when he *can't even swim that well*!'

'Oh, for heaven's sake—do you really think I would have placed him in any danger? I've known Stavros all his life, and he swims like an eel!' he snapped. 'I've been with them all morning, and apparently you all had dinner together last night. They've been getting along famously. If you hadn't overslept you could have seen that for yourself.' His expression darkened. 'What I want to know is why he can't damned well swim in the first place?'

'Because...'

'Because *what*, Laura?' he queried archly.

'Because—' Oh, what was the point in hiding anything from him? 'Well, the lessons were expensive…' Her voice tailed away as she realised he was looking at her in disbelief.

'Expensive?' he repeated incredulously.

She thought he sounded as if he were trying out a new and unknown word. But how *could* he understand what it was like to have to make every penny count when he had spent a life with an abundance of wealth?

'He has football coaching at the weekends instead,' she justified. 'And I couldn't afford everything.'

'So here we have my son, the pauper,' he said bitterly. 'A Karantinos heir living on the breadline!'

Laura swallowed, suddenly realising how exhausted he looked—as if he hadn't had a wink of sleep all night. His black eyes were hooded and tired, and the dark shadow at his jaw suggested that he might not yet have shaved. The expensively dressed Greek billionaire was a world away from this barefoot and elemental-looking man in faded jeans and T-shirt who stood in front of her.

It seemed all too disturbingly intimate and familiar—a glimpse of the old Constantine—and Laura shrank back, suddenly and dangerously aware of his proximity and the fact that while he was fully dressed she was wearing very little. Nothing but a very short wrap over an equally short night-dress that barely came to the middle of her bare thigh. And from the sudden tightening of his features the realisation had begun to dawn on him at precisely the same moment.

Without another word, Laura turned and walked out of the room and back along the corridor to her own—but to her horror and shameful excitement, she realised that Constantine was right behind her.

'No,' she whispered ineffectively, as he shut the door behind him and she felt his warm breath on her neck.

'Oh, yes,' he said grimly, turning her round as if she were a mannequin in a store window. 'You should not walk around the house half-naked if you don't want this particular outcome—nor make big eyes at me and allow your body to tremble with such obvious hunger whenever you come near me.'

Afterwards, she'd try to tell herself that she had done everything to resist him—but that would be a complete lie. She did nothing. Nothing but stare up at him, her parched lips parting with unashamed yearning, a tiny little whimper of desire escaping from them as he moved closer still. And then it was too late. His kiss was like dynamite, his touch the fire which made it combust—and Laura went up in flames.

'*Oh*,' she moaned, clawing at his shoulders as he caught her by the waist and brought her up hard against the aroused cradle of his desire, so that she could feel the shockingly unfamiliar hard ridge of him pressing up against her through his jeans.

With an uncharacteristic disregard for foreplay, he slid up her nightdress and this time found her bare and ready for him, giving a little groan of delight as he tangled his fingers in her hair and then greedily delved inside her honeyed moistness as she gasped out her fevered response. He closed his eyes helplessly as she swayed against him, her hips moving with sudden instinct against his fingers.

Laura clung to him, her love-starved body hungry for his kiss and for everything else she knew he could give her. His fingers were moving purposefully between her legs now, and he was driving his mouth down on hers in a kiss which quite literally took her breath away—a kiss she never wanted to end.

And then she felt a change taking place in her body; the rhythm of his fingers was changing pace—quickening against her blossoming heat. She felt the wild beat of her heart—the momentary lull before she tumbled over—her body spasming helplessly against his hand, his kiss silencing her little gasps of fulfilment as she slumped weakly against him until the last of her orgasm died away.

'Constantine,' she breathed eventually, her cheeks flushed and her heart beating fast. 'Oh, Constantine.'

'I want you,' he whispered fiercely into her ear. He guided her hand to lie over the achingly hard ridge in his jeans. 'Feel how much I want you.'

And she wanted him, too. But it was broad daylight in the middle of the morning, and she had responsibilities which were far more urgent that the siren call of her body. 'N-Not now…' The words stumbled out of her mouth. 'A-And not here. We can't. You know we can't.'

Through the dark, erotic mists of his desire came her unsteady voice of reason. At first he tried to ignore it—but something at its very heart made Constantine still and pull his lips away from hers, to stare down into the flushed confusion of her face, the tumbled gold of her unbrushed hair.

His heart was thundering so powerfully he could barely think, let alone speak. 'You think that it is right to deny me pleasure now that you have taken your own? Is that right?'

Dumbly, she shook her head.

Fuelled by a savage wave of frustration, he felt the slow flare of anger begin to burn. 'You think you can keep tantalising me and that I will be like a tame puppy who will just keep trotting behind you and taking whatever it is that you dish out to me? Letting you turn me down, time and time again—so that I can't sleep at night for thinking about your pale, curved body? Taking me so far with your sweet, soft promise and then acting outraged? Is that what men usually let you do, Laura?'

She was too busy catching her breath to rise to the taunt.

'Have you become a *tease*, Laura?' he persisted.

Her lips were trembling, 'No. *No*.'

'Just a woman who promises so much, who lets a man touch her so intimately and then freezes up? If that isn't your definition of a tease, then I'd like to know what is.'

Frustratedly, she shook her head—knowing that he spoke nothing but the truth. She was acting like a naïve little virgin around him, when they both knew she was anything but. The kind of woman who would let a man only go so far... Was that because she thought that her continued resistance to full-on sex might make him respect her? When just one look at the contemptuous mask of his features proved that respect was the very last thing he was feeling?

And what of her *own* desires? Hadn't she been living like a nun for the past eight years? Though it had not felt like denial because no one had moved her to passion. But Constantine had. Constantine still did. It was all there for the taking if only she could accept that it would just be no-strings sex.

'I'm not saying I don't want you—how could I when I've just proved the very opposite?' she whispered. 'Just not now and not here—when Alex might come back from the pool and start looking for me.'

His unyielding expression did not alter. 'So, when?'

Laura could have wept. How matter-of-fact he sounded. It had taken a lot for her to say that, and yet it was as if the significance of her declaration was irrelevant and all he wanted was to pin her down to a time and a place. Her breath came out in a shuddering sigh, but she knew that she couldn't back out of it now, even if she wanted to.

'Come to me tonight,' she whispered. 'Late. When the house is quiet and when I know for sure that Alex is asleep.'

He felt the urgent leap of anticipation at his groin and he stared deep into the storm clouds of her eyes. Taking her slender waist between his hands, he bent his head to graze his lips over hers, feeling her tremble as he did so. Had she learnt somewhere along the way that a woman's most effective weapon was resistance? Was that why she had applied it so effectively, making him desire her with a power which set his blood on fire for her?

And yet with Laura it did not feel like a game she was playing with him in an attempt to ensnare him. This felt real—as if she was fighting herself as well as fighting him.

'I shall spend the whole day thinking about it, *agape mou*,' he murmured. 'Imagining you naked in my arms. Pinned beneath my body as I drive into you over and over again. Yes, I will come to you tonight.' He smiled as he brushed an indolent finger over her trembling lips. 'Now, hurry up and get dressed before I change my mind about waiting.'

With a mounting feeling of disbelief, Laura watched as he left the room, hugging her flimsy little wrap closer to her still flushed and trembling body.

She felt calmer after she'd showered and dressed and pulled on the floral pinafore Demetra had given her to wear. Not the most flattering garment in the world—but that wasn't supposed to be its function, was it?

She stared at her rather drab image in the mirror. It was stupid to feel ashamed of waitressing when it was a job she had done with pride and efficiency during many periods of her adult life. But this felt different, and maybe that was because it *was*. She was going to have to wait on the father of her child and pretend that he meant nothing to her.

Shutting the door quietly behind her, Laura went outside to find Alex splashing around with Stavros in the shallow end of an enormous swimming pool.

'Mum!' he yelled. 'Look! Stavros is teaching me breaststroke!'

Laura smiled as the seal-dark wet head of the student emerged from the water. 'Thank you, Stavros.'

The student grinned as he gestured for Alex to come forward. 'I like to teach, and he shows promise. Young children learn quickly. Come, Alex, show your mama what you can do.'

Alex doggy-paddled over to the edge of the pool and stared up at her, and Laura's heart turned over as she saw the look of pure joy on his little face. 'Don't get tired, will you, darling?' she said.

'*Mum!*'

'Did you have breakfast?'

'Yes, I had it with Constantine.' Alex grinned. 'We had yoghurt—with *honey*! And Constantine and me went and picked oranges from the tree and then we squeezed them!'

She gazed down at him, thinking how easily her son had slotted into life here—already. *And* how easily he seemed to be slotting into a relationship with Constantine, too. Why, he must have felt as if he had landed in heaven with all the space and beauty which surrounded him

The dark flicker of fear invaded her heart once more. Fear that Alex might just fall in love with Greece and the powerful man who had fathered him—and might not want to return with her to their grey and penny-pinching life back in England...

'Lovely, darling,' she managed to say. 'Well, I'm supposed to be working, so I'd better go and see what Demetra wants me to do.'

Laura made her way to the kitchen to find Demetra, who seemed to have assumed the role of mother hen. First she insisted that Laura sit outside and eat some bread and honey, and drink some of the thick, strong coffee.

'You are too thin,' Demetra commented as she pushed a bowl of bread towards her. 'A woman needs her strength.'

Tell me about it, thought Laura wryly, as she sliced a peach into gleaming rose-tinged slices. But mental strength was surely just as important as the physical kind— and you couldn't build *that* up with bread and honey! But she felt oddly moved by the older woman's kindness— because it had been so long since someone had fussed over her like this.

And at least working was therapeutic—it was hard to stay troubled when your fingers were busy chopping salads and stuffing vine leaves. Demetra showed her how to make a sweet pastry dish which was soaked in lemon syrup after baking—as well as a pudding studded with nuts and raisins and flavoured with cinnamon and cloves.

Laura leaned back against the range. 'Where did you learn how to cook like this, Demetra?'

'Oh, I have cooked all my life,' answered Demetra simply. 'First for my husband and then for my living. You see, I was widowed when Stavros was just a baby, and so I came here to work for the Karantinos family. They have been good to me. And Kyrios Constantine is a good man,' she added fiercely. 'He used to fish with my husband—and when he died he put Stavros through school and university and made sure the boy wanted for nothing.'

The housekeeper's words of praise for Constantine preoccupied Laura as she began to lay the table on the terrace, beneath a canopy of leaves. But the last thing she needed was to hear praise lavished on him. She wanted to put him out of her mind—at least until tonight.

'Do you know, I could stay here all day watching you do that?' murmured a deep voice from the shadows, and Laura whirled round to find Constantine at the other end of the terrace, his black eyes fixed on her. Clearly fresh from the shower, with tiny droplets of water bejewelling the black hair, he had changed from jeans and T-shirt into dark trousers and a thin silk shirt, and he had shaved, too.

'How long have you been standing there?' she accused, her heart beginning to race with a ridiculous excitement.

He began walking towards her, his progress made slow by an exquisitely painful arousal. 'Long enough to see that delightfully old-fashioned pinafore dress stretched tight over the delectable curve of your bottom,' he murmured. 'Making me want to touch it again, quite urgently.'

Laura sent an agonised glance in the direction of the kitchen, even though the rattle of china told her that Demetra was not within earshot. 'Constantine, don't. Please. Somebody might hear.'

His black eyes mocked her. 'Ah, Laura! You see how already we are colluding like lovers—even though we are not yet lovers? For that pleasure I must wait—and I am not a man who is used to waiting.'

'No, I can believe that,' she said quietly, holding the tray in front of her as if it were a shield.

He lowered his voice until it was nothing but a silken

caress which whispered over her skin. 'Do you know that I feel as a man in prison must feel, ticking off the seconds and the minutes and the hours?'

Laura swallowed. 'Constantine—'

'So that the whole day seems stretched out in front of me like a piece of elastic,' he continued inexorably. 'Which is tightening unbearably—tighter and tighter—until the time when it snaps and I can once more feel your lips on mine and your honeyed heat as it welcomes me into your body.'

'Stop it,' she whispered as the siren song of desire began a slow pulsing through her veins 'Please, stop it. Or how will I compose myself in front of the others?'

'You didn't think through the potential problems of making such an erotic date with destiny, did you?' he taunted.

She hadn't counted on being on such an erotic knife-edge, no. 'Do you think your father's going to ask me anything?'

'If he does, then just answer his questions truthfully,' he said, his whole mood suddenly sobering. 'If you think you can manage that.'

'You're…making it sound as if you think I'm a liar,' said Laura unsteadily, trying to read his expression—but it would have been easier to have sought some sort of meaning from a statue.

Constantine shook his head. 'I haven't quite decided what you are,' he said softly. 'Or just what your agenda is.'

Her heart slammed against her ribcage. 'Who says I have an agenda?'

'Women always do—it's in their genetic make-up.'

'You're a cynic, Constantine.'

'No, *agape mou*,' he contradicted softly. 'I am simply a very rich man who has seen female ambition in its every form. And you—of all women—have the opportunity to try to take me for everything you can get your hands on.'

'You think that I'd do that?' she demanded breathlessly.

'I told you—I haven't made up my mind yet,' he returned.

And yet Laura had confounded every one of his expectations of her. Her refusal to marry him and her stubborn insistence on coming here to work instead had left him feeling unsettled. After a lifetime spent dodging matrimonial commitment to some of the world's most eligible women, he had assumed that this humble waitress would leap at the chance of being a rich man's wife—yet she had done the very opposite. So was she simply being devious, or principled?

'Now—if you'll excuse me—I have some business calls I need to make before lunch.' His eyes glittered with erotic intent. 'And roll on midnight, my stormy-eyed little temptress, so that we can at last finish off what we've started.'

For a moment after he'd gone Laura stood rooted to the spot—unable to believe how a man could switch so quickly from desire to distrust and then back to desire again. She finished laying the table for lunch, and then went to help Alex get ready.

'Is Constantine's daddy very old?' he wanted to know, as he wriggled into a brand-new T-shirt.

'I believe so, darling—and he hasn't been too well recently, so you must be well-behaved.' Surprisingly, Alex let her attempt to tame his dark waves into shape and, stepping back, her eyes shone with maternal pride as she looked at him. 'But I know you will.'

The lunch table looked beautiful—with little pots of purple and white flowers dotted everywhere—and Stavros and Alex sat at their places, waiting until Constantine appeared with his father. Laura watched as they made slow progress across the terrace, the old man leaning heavily on a stick.

He's so *old*, realised Laura suddenly. Why, he must be in his mid-eighties. Which meant that he… She frowned as she worked out what age he'd have been when Constantine was born. Fifty, at least. Had his wife also been elderly? she wondered. Was that why she'd succumbed to a bout of pneumonia?

Kyrios Karantinos was, as Constantine had said, very frail—but it was easy to see how handsome he must once have been. He had the most amazing bone structure, and Laura found herself wondering with a pang whether Alex would look a little like this when he was an old man. Whether Constantine would.

And whether she would still be around to see it.

The faded eyes looked her up and down as he waved Constantine away and looked at Laura. Was it wrong to play the part of being some kind of waitress in this elderly man's house? she wondered, as a sudden pang of guilt washed over her. But it *wasn't* a part, was it? She *was* a waitress. This was far more honest than turning up here as Constantine's new bride, married to a man who seemed to alternate between despising and desiring her—now, that really *would* have been a living lie. And one that any father would surely veto.

Nervously, Laura smoothed down the front of her pinafore dress. 'I'm very pleased to meet you, Kyrios Karantinos,' she said.

'My son tells me that you met in England?'

'Yes, sir.'

'And that you persuaded him to let you come and work here for the summer?'

'That's right. It seemed a great opportunity to give my son a holiday.'

There was a momentary pause before he gestured towards the curly-haired little boy in his new shorts and T-shirt. 'And this is your little boy?'

'Yes, this is Alex.'

The faded eyes were now turned in the direction of the child, and for a moment Laura thought that she saw them narrow. But the moment passed, and slowly he sat down and began asking Alex about his morning. To Laura's delight and pride her son began to chatter away. He began to tell the old man about his swimming lesson, and she longed to stay and listen, but Constantine was raising his hand to get her attention.

Her cheeks burned as she met the mocking look in his black eyes and registered the arrogant tone in his voice as he clipped out an order for wine. He's enjoying this, she thought to herself suddenly as she hurried out towards the kitchen. He's enjoying rubbing in my subservient status.

She tried to tell herself not to be affected by Constantine's sardonic scorn, but that was easier said than done. When he gestured arrogantly for the bread basket she found herself wanting to hurl its contents at his hateful head. Or to tip the cool yoghurt and cucumber dish of *tzatziki* all over his lap.

In fact, she was so busy keeping everyone's glasses filled and bringing out dish after dish that Laura had no real opportunity to take in what was going on—much as she longed to listen to what Alex was saying to his grandfather, or to see whether the old man showed any sign of guessing who the little boy really was. And it felt peculiar to be serving her own son his lunch in the guise of a waitress.

Never had she felt more of an outsider than she did during that seemingly endless meal—it was as if she was an observer, watching a play unfold before her. As if she had no real place anywhere.

And wasn't there a rather frozen lack of communication between Constantine and his own father? As if the two men tolerated each other rather than loving one another? Is that the kind of role model Constantine is planning to provide for Alex? she wondered, feeling suddenly fearful. That of emotional containment?

But at least Alex himself seemed to have come into his own, blossoming in a way she had never seen him doing before. He was lapping up all the attention, she realised. From Constantine, from his father, and from young Stavros, too. *Because he wasn't used to the company of men.* For the first time she could see how limiting his life must be, living with two women in a cramped apartment above a village shop.

And all the time she was aware of Constantine watching the scene too, his shuttered black eyes hidden behind the dark lashes, his gaze drifting to the animated features of the little boy. Had he sat at that very table and chattered away like that when he was Alex's age? she wondered.

She watched as he began to peel an orange for his son, her gaze drawn inexorably to the strong fingers as they pulled away petal-shaped segments of the peel. Shadows fell from the high-angled slash of his cheekbones and the sensual curve of his lips had relaxed into a half-smile. And then he suddenly looked up, and the ebony spotlight of his gaze swept over her, and she found herself flushing as he raised his glass in her direction.

'Can you fetch me some more ice for my water?' he

questioned carelessly, and Laura's colour heightened as she nodded and went off to the kitchen in search of some.

He watched her go. Watched the high, tempting curves of her buttocks thrusting against the dowdy clothes, and once again he felt his heart-rate soar. What was it this plain little creature had which made his body ache like this? he asked himself bitterly. Was it because she was the mother of his child? Or because she was the only virgin he had ever bedded? Perhaps his desire for her was stronger than anything he had ever known simply because she had refused him time and time again. More importantly, would this terrible hunger cease once he had possessed her? His lips curved. Of course it would. As if someone like her could hold his attention for more than one night!

Laura returned, carrying the ice, and bent to put some in his glass, temptingly aware of the tantalising warmth of his body and the faint trace of his musky scent. Was he silently laughing at the image she presented as she served him—and when those black eyes swept over her in insolent assessment what did they see? A too-slight woman serving drinks in an unflattering floral pinafore dress? A mother who had willingly put herself in the role of outcast by waiting at her lover's table?

Laura wondered if that was all they saw. Perhaps his gaze was perceptive enough to delve beneath the surface and guess at her feelings of apprehension and vulnerability. Was he feeling quietly triumphant as he anticipated the assignation she had so willingly agreed to tonight—and might he use it against her? *To do what?*

She thought of all the empty promises she had made to herself—that she would not succumb to the overwhelming chemistry which still sizzled between them. That she would protect her heart from pain by not getting close to him in any way.

And then she thought of their midnight assignation, closing her eyes as her body registered an automatic thrill of anticipation—despite the damning quality of the words he had whispered. What had they been? *Ah, yes. To finish off what they'd started.*

Laura bit her lip as she carried out a dish of almonds to the table. Was there any scenario more potentially heart-breaking than the one which lay ahead of her?

CHAPTER NINE

A CRACK of light slanted across the floor as the door opened, and Laura held her breath as she saw the dark and formidable shape of Constantine standing silhouetted there. If he thought she was sleeping, would he creep away again? she wondered. Would he remember that she had been working and perhaps might need her rest? Spare her this sensual ordeal which she suspected might open the door to a terrible kind of heartache? And yet her heart was pounding so hard that she was certain he must be able to hear its frantic beat.

A low laugh beside the bed put paid to her half-hearted hopes. 'Surely you don't expect me to believe you are asleep do you, *ghlikos mou*?' he questioned softly.

She heard the rasp of a zip, and then the soft thump of something slithering to the ground—presumably his jeans—before a rush of air to her skin as he peeled the sheet away from her body and climbed into bed. Laura trembled as she felt that first contact with his warm, muscular flesh.

'You're...*naked*,' she breathed.

'What did you expect?' With comfortable assurance he hooked his arms around her and drew her close, the glitter of his eyes discernible in the moonlight, his breath warm on her face. 'Ah...perhaps you wanted to watch me strip?'

'I....' His easy provocation left her feeling cheated and out of her depth. *He does this kind of thing all the time,* she reminded herself—*and he has no idea that it's been eight long years since you slept with a man. This man.* Had she mistakenly hoped that there might be some kind of wooing, and that he might be gentle with her? Perhaps taking her tenderly in his arms and tossing her a few compliments, before beginning a slow lovemaking? Was she *crazy*?

'Meanwhile, you...are most definitely *not* naked,' he murmured, as he skated his hand down over one cotton-covered hip, and she heard the faint deprecation in his voice. 'Shame on you, Laura—I cannot believe you always wear something this unflattering in bed when you make an assignation with your lover.'

She guessed that now was not the time to tell him that this was her first such assignation. But she realised that Constantine hadn't been expecting a reply—his question had merely been the precursor to skimming the nightie up and over her head, and tossing it over the side of the bed like a flag of surrender. She shivered as her nakedness was revealed.

'Cold?' he murmured, as his lips found the line of her jaw and began to whisper along its curve.

'N-no.'

'Surely not scared?'

Scared? She was *terrified*—because didn't sex play havoc with a woman's emotions? And weren't hers already see-sawing their way towards chaos and a terrible feeling of vulnerability? But she shook her head, unwilling to admit to fear or doubt or anything else which might put her at even more of a disadvantage in his arms.

'Good.' He lifted his hand to smooth some of the fine mass of pale hair away from her face. 'You see, you have made me wait too long for this, Laura. Much too long... longer than any other woman would have dared or been able to. You have driven me half mad with temptation— do you realise that?' His voice was unsteady as he drove his mouth down on hers with a hunger so fierce that it made his body shudder, and her hands reached up to cling to him so that even his taunting words about other women were forgotten beneath the power of his kiss.

Constantine groaned as her lips opened eagerly to welcome him and he felt the softness of her breasts. His fingers skimmed her body, reacquainting themselves with all its curves and secret places, luxuriating in the soft, silken feel of her skin—and he groaned again.

He had found the delay before getting into her bed almost unendurable—their snatched and teasing foreplay something he had not experienced since he was a teenager—and it had been compounded by the fact that she was the mother of his child. For once his feelings were less than straightforward—she had captured his imagination as well as his desire. But in the sweetness of the moment all that was forgotten, and now she was so compliant beneath his embrace that Constantine knew this was all going to happen very quickly. Too quickly.

And perhaps Laura sensed it too, because she suddenly pulled away from him, her eyes huge in her face.

'Contraception?' she whispered.

'You?'

'I don't...have anything.'

Swearing softly in Greek, he reached blindly for the jeans he'd left on the floor until he found a condom.

Gingerly he slid it on, and then pulled her soft body back into his arms. 'Let's hope it's a little more reliable than last time,' he drawled.

Laura stiffened as the impact of his words hit home, and half tried to pull away from him. 'That's a hateful thing to say.'

'You want to hide from the truth? Is that it?'

'I think there's a time and a place for everything—and that remark was wrong on just about every level.'

He gave a brief half-smile. 'You dare to scold me, *ghlikos mou*?' Before she could answer, he tipped her chin upwards and stared down at her with erotic intent. 'But then you dare to do many things which surprise me, Laura. Now, where was I? Was it here?' He lowered his head until his mouth found the lobe of her ear and whispered over its plump little oval. 'Or here?' His lips moved to hers, felt them tremble, and that involuntary little shudder moved him more than it should have done.

He kissed silent her little cries, his greedy fingers exploring her body with a thoroughness which left her gasping—finding her most vulnerable places and tantalising her until he felt her squirm with impatient longing. And her fervour filled him with a strange kind of disquiet, even while it set his senses on fire. 'Are you always this eager?' he murmured.

'Are you?' she parried.

No, he thought suddenly. No, he was not—but then this was the only woman who had had his child grow within her body. 'That doesn't answer my question,' he said unevenly.

No, it didn't—and while Laura knew that there was no earthly reason why she should respond, instinct told her that her answer would please him. And why not please him when he was in her arms and in her bed and soon to be in her body?

'I am only this eager with you,' she said, her voice dipping a little with sexual shyness. 'For you are the only lover I have ever known.'

There was a moment of disbelief while he sucked in a ragged breath, and suddenly the power of that thought made him feel momentarily weak—or as weak as Constantine was ever capable of being. 'The *only* one?' he demanded.

'Yes. And now will you please shut up about it? Or you'll give me a complex.'

He groaned as she kissed him back, boldly tracing her soft and seeking lips over every inch of his body, and then he gave a low laugh as he took her soft breast in his hand and stroked it.

He held back until he could hold back no longer, and then he touched her once again between the sweet haven of her thighs and felt her quiver with pleasure. Tearing his lips away from hers, he stared down into her face for an infinitesimal moment before—with one long, delicious stroke—he filled her and let out a long moan of pleasure.

The feel of him inside her again after so long was a sweet shock—but Laura barely had time to accommodate him, or to savour the sensation of Constantine moving within her, thrusting deep into her body and deep into her heart. Because all too quickly she was spiralling once more towards that dizzy destination he'd led her to that very afternoon, when he had brought her to orgasm with his fingers. But this was something else. This was the real thing. *He* was the real thing. Her heart gave a sudden lurch in time with her limbs.

'Oh, *Constantine*,' she cried, and she felt tears spilling from beneath her eyelids. '*Constantine*!'

Smothering her little gasps with his lips, he felt her

bucking uncontrollably beneath him, and the spasming of her body sent his own pleasure hurtling right off the radar. He waited until he could wait no longer—until his orgasm took him under completely, instead of his more usual controlled riding it out, like a wave. And the unexpectedness of that surrender momentarily took his breath away.

Afterwards, he felt as though she had taken something from him, but he wasn't quite sure what. Abruptly he rolled away from her, and lay beside her on the rumpled sheets, staring at the moon-dappled ceiling, waiting for her words—the words that women always said at moments like these, when they were at their weakest. Praise, adoration and undying love—Constantine had heard them all in his time. Words which were his due and yet words he often scorned because of their transparent predictability. Yet Laura said nothing.

He turned his head to look at her—she was lying perfectly still, with her eyes closed and her pale hair spread out like a fine cloud across the pillow. She was so still she might almost have been sleeping—the fading gleam of tears drying on her heated cheeks the only clue as to what had just taken place. She must have sensed that his gaze was on her, yet still she did not open her eyes and look at him.

Which made the next step easy, didn't it? An early exit from her bed—which was what he had planned on making all along. Besides, he preferred sleeping on his own once his passion had been spent, and the cloying emotions of waking up with a woman always left him cold. So why the hell was he lying here in a state of indolent bliss, heavy-limbed and unwilling to stir?

For a moment Laura didn't move, couldn't think—her equilibrium thrown off kilter by what had just happened between them. She found herself biting back inappropriate words—telling him that sex with him was one of the most glorious things which had ever happened to her, and so was he. Telling him that she had been a rash and stupid fool to have turned down his offer of marriage and please could she reconsider? But as her shattered senses returned to something approaching normality she knew she had to put some distance between them in order to protect herself.

Because sex could make you feel too close to a man—it could make you start concocting all kinds of emotional fantasies about that man. And hadn't she just been doing exactly that? Imagining herself half way in love with him? She should never forget that the man in question had a heart of stone—why, he'd moved as far away from her as possible as soon as their bodies had stilled. And hadn't he made this 'assignation' of theirs sound completely unemotional—mechanical, even? Well, then, pride should make her do the same.

'I think...I think that perhaps you'd better go now,' she suggested huskily.

Constantine, who had been mentally preparing himself to do exactly that, stilled. '*Go*?' he echoed in soft disbelief.

She risked opening her eyes then, and wished she hadn't—for in the bright moonlight Constantine lay on the bed like a beautiful dark statue, with the rumpled sheet which lay carelessly over one narrow hip only just covering his manhood.

Laura swallowed. 'Well, yes. I mean...Alex might come in early and I don't... Well, I don't want him to find us in bed together.'

'How very admirable of you, Laura,' he murmured, but inside his feelings were at war. He felt anger that she—

she—should be the one to eject Constantine Karantinos from her bed—and yet this went hand in hand with an undeniable and fierce approval that she should demonstrate such sound morality around his impressionable young son.

He pushed the sheet back from his inconveniently hardening body and watched the way that her nipples were peaking in response. He saw the movement of her throat as she swallowed down her desire, and the way her eyes were now drawn irresistibly to his groin. 'Though if you continue to lie there looking at me like that, then I might just change my mind,' he said thickly.

The statement—or was it a question?—hung on the air as she saw the sudden tension return to his body, and Laura's tongue snaked around her lips, her thighs parting by a fraction as she shifted uncomfortably on the bed.

Constantine rolled over. Kissed her nipple. Heard her gasp as he stroked between her legs and then slicked on a condom. Suddenly she was urging him inside her, and it seemed like only seconds before he felt her spasming helplessly around him and he followed her almost immediately, his mouth pressed against her shoulder as he bit out his fulfilment. But he withdrew from her as soon as the last sweet wave shuddered away, moving from the bed with an elegant grace as he began to pull on his clothes.

'Constantine—'

Zipping up his jeans, he looked down at the flushed and startled expression on her face. 'Mmm?'

'Maybe...' Her voice was tentative. 'Maybe I might change my mind this time. About you staying. As long as you leave early.'

Although he was now on the much more familiar ground of a woman trying to inveigle him back into her bed, Constantine narrowed his eyes with a slowly smouldering anger. Did she really think he was the kind of man who would pander to her whims—the kind of man to be played with as a kitten played with a mouse? Wasn't she in danger of over-estimating her appeal to him?

His mouth twisted. 'I don't think so, *agape mou*. Alex is asleep down the hall—and until he knows that I am his father, then I don't think it's a good idea if he finds me in your bed, do you? Sweet dreams,' he said softly, and turned and left the room without another word.

For a moment Laura just lay there, watching the door close behind him, her body still glowing with the aftermath of pleasure but her heart aching with a terrible kind of pain. Had she mistakenly thought that sex might bring about some sort of closure? Maybe give her some guidance about how she was going to extricate herself and Alex from this situation while causing the least amount of hurt all round?

If so, then she had been hugely mistaken. Because behind all the passion she had felt Constantine's bitterness, and the knowledge that it could take her to a dark, dark place.

She must have drifted off to sleep, because when she opened her eyes she was surprised to find it was six o'clock. The house was still silent and for a moment she lay there, reliving the night before and its horribly unsatisfactory ending. She showered and dressed, and spent ten minutes tugging the rumpled bed back into some sort of order before going to the other end of the corridor and poking her head around Alex's door.

He was fast asleep, his dark lashes feathering down into two sooty arcs, the faint colour to his skin an indication that he had been playing in the sunshine. He looked really contented, she thought with a sudden glow—and her heart felt a little lighter as she went down to the empty kitchen and made herself a coffee.

Taking the cup outside, she went to stand at the top of the stone steps at the end of the garden and stood looking out to sea, where the giant crimson globe of the sun was rising up over the milky horizon. It was such a beautiful place, she thought wistfully—and yet it seemed to have its own shadows and secrets. Though maybe every place on earth did.

Later, she was busy constructing a giant plate of fruit for breakfast, while Demetra pounded away at some dough and bemoaned the fact that the village no longer had a bakery, when Laura heard a rapid clicking sound and looked up.

'What's that?' she questioned.

Demetra paused. 'Oh, the helicopter.' She shrugged. 'It will be Kyrios Constantine, going to Athens.'

'To…to *Athens*?' questioned Laura shakily, her heart crashing uncomfortably against her ribcage. She told herself that it was unreasonable of her to expect him to inform her of his movements. But didn't last night's lovemaking entitle her to the common courtesy of him at least coming to say goodbye? She could see Demetra looking at her curiously, and found herself struggling to say something suitably conventional. What would a casual servant say at such a time? 'Er…the pilot lives on the island, does he?'

'Oh, he needs no pilot,' answered Demetra. 'Kyrios Constantine flies the helicopter himself!'

'And is he…working in Athens?' questioned Laura

'Work, yes—and probably women, too.' Demetra's eyes crinkled conspiratorially. 'Always the women—they flock to Kyrios Constantine like ants around the honeypot.'

The housekeeper's words made her hand jerk, and the

fruit knife she was holding inadvertently nicked her thumb. Laura quickly put it down as a small spot of crimson blood welled up and began to drip onto the wooden table.

CHAPTER TEN

'YOU'VE cut your thumb,' observed Constantine softly.

'Oh, it's nothing.'

'Nothing?' he murmured. 'Come here—let me see.'

Laura squirmed as he took the injured digit in his hand and even that innocent contact sent her senses spiralling. Earlier that day he had flown back, after spending three nights in Athens, and while she was ridiculously pleased to see him she couldn't dispel her terrible aching insecurity and jealousy at the thought of what he might have been doing there.

They were sitting by the edge of the sea, on a beach more beautiful than any beach she could ever have imagined—just her, Alex and Constantine, who had insisted that she and her son both needed to see more of the island, especially as today was officially her day off.

Alex had spent the morning playing with a magnificent sandcastle which his father had constructed while demonstrating a sweet kind of patience which had made Laura's heart turn over with an aching wistfulness. Because it was like glimpsing the sun appearing from behind a thick, dark cloud. This was the Constantine who usually lay hidden behind that formidable exterior—the one he rarely allowed people to see. The side he had shown her all those years ago…the side which had made him all to easy to love—and still did.

They had just eaten salads and cheese for lunch, and now their son was lying in the cool shade of a rock, fast asleep—a cute cotton hat shielding his little face from the occasional sand-fly. It felt strange to be out like a normal family—without her floral pinafore dress and the subtle sense of subservience which she adopted whenever she put it on. And strange too to be in the company of the man she had not seen since he had left her room after that passionate night of lovemaking.

When he had left without a word about why or where he was going, she reminded herself.

'How did you do it?' questioned Constantine as he continued with his mock-examination of her thumb, which was raising her heart-rate significantly.

'I…I cut it on a fruit knife.'

'Clumsy of you, Laura.'

'Yes.' She wanted to tell him not to touch her like that—yet she knew that such words would sound like hysterical nonsense, because to the outside world it would look like nothing more than an innocent assessment of her thumb. But to Laura it felt as if he were trailing sizzling fire where he made contact. As if her nerve-endings became instantly raw and clamouring wherever his fingertips brushed against them.

And yet conversely she wanted him to touch her in a far more inappropriate way altogether. To have him pull her into his arms—to at least give *some* indication that they'd actually been lovers. But of course he did not touch her, and Laura tried to tell herself it was because Alex was nearby.

'So…what were you doing in Athens?' she questioned suddenly, even though she had vowed she would not.

For a moment Constantine didn't answer as he let her hand go, an odd, mocking kind of smile curving the corners of his lips. 'I don't think that's any of your business, do you?'

It was the response of her worst nightmares, and it made all her uncertainties bubble to the surface. Heart pounding with fear, she glanced quickly over at Alex, but he was fast asleep, worn out by the morning and oblivious to the low, urgent tones of his parents. 'Did you go straight from my bed to another's?'

His black eyes sent her a mocking challenge. 'Why? Is that the kind of behaviour you normally indulge in yourself?'

She clenched her hands into tiny fists. 'You know very well that you're the only person I've ever slept with!'

On hearing this for a second time, Constantine felt his heart accelerate into a thundering kind of triumphant beat. He was Greek, and he was pure alpha-male, and he would have been lying if her declaration hadn't thrilled him to every fibre of his being—but he was damned if he would let it show.

'Ah, if only I could say the same, *agape mou*,' he sighed regretfully.

Tears stung her eyes. 'Why do you delight in hurting me?' she demanded, realising too late how vulnerable that made her sound. But Constantine didn't seem to have noticed.

'Don't you think that hurt is an inevitable part of a relationship?' he returned with a shrug. 'Of *all* relationships?'

She disregarded his careless use of the word 'relationship,' because the clue was in the emphasised word and Laura seized on it. 'Is that what happened with you, Constantine? You got hurt?'

'I've seen how women can hurt and manipulate, yes.'

'Girlfriends, you mean?'

'No, not *girlfriends*,' he answered scornfully.

'You mean…your mother?' she guessed, as she remembered the odd, strained look on his face when he'd mentioned her.

He shrugged in affirmation but didn't bother to reply. Hopefully she might take the hint and quit interrogating him.

'What happened?'

Did she never learn when to leave well enough alone—that her probing questions were unwelcome? 'What happened happened a long time ago,' he snapped. 'So forget it.'

Laura leaned a little closer. 'But I don't want to forget it. This is Alex's grandmother we're talking about, and one day he may want to know. Won't you tell me, Constantine? Please?'

What was it about her softly spoken question that sparked a need to reply—*to confide about things he had never told another?* he wondered, raking his dark hair back from his brow in frustration. He was a man who never confided, who was strong for everyone. The buck stopped with Constantine and it had done for many years, but now words came spilling from his lips like a stream of dark poison.

'She was years younger than my father—decades, in fact. A beautiful, fragile beauty who bewitched him—and because he was almost fifty when they married her youth and her beauty hit him like a hurricane. When a man has never known passion until late in life it can take him over like a fever.' He shrugged. 'He neglected everything in pursuit of a love she was ill-equipped to return—but then she was incapable of loving anyone but herself.'

'Even you?' said Laura slowly.

Her question broke into the tumult of his thoughts, but Constantine was in too far to stop now. 'Even me,' he answered, and the admission was like a hammer blow—for was there not something almost shameful about admitting that the most fundamental bond of all, between mother and child, had simply not existed in their case? But the precise side of Constantine's nature meant that he needed to attempt to define it.

'She was one of those people who did not seem to be of this earth—she was too fey and too delicate, and she did not look after herself,' he continued. 'She partied and drank wine instead of eating—smoked cigarettes instead of breathing in the pure Greek air. And when she died her enchantment still did not end—for my father went to pieces. He became one of those men who are obsessed by a ghost and who live in a past which only really exists in their own imagination. It was only when I took over the business properly that I was able to see just how badly he had let things go.'

Laura stared at his hard and beautiful features, transformed now into a mask hardened by pain and memory. So even his father had not been there for him—which explained the lack of closeness between the two men. 'I'm so sorry,' she said simply.

He turned, angry with her, but far angrier with himself for having unleashed some of the dark secrets of his soul. 'I do not want your sympathy,' he snapped.

'But I think that—'

'And neither do I want your advice—no matter how well intentioned! You are a woman from humble circumstances who knows nothing of this life of privilege which you have entered solely because you are the mother of my son! And you would do well to remember your place here!'

Laura reached for her sunglasses and rammed them down over her eyes before he could see the tears which were brimming up behind her lids. *Remember your place here.* How cheap did that make her feel? His words were barely any different from her own thoughts about them occupying different worlds—but, oh, how it hurt to hear them flung at her with such venom. He didn't like women, she realised—and, while it was easy to see why, it wasn't going to change, was it? Nothing *she* said would ever change it.

She saw Alex begin to stir—had their low but angry words wakened him? she wondered guiltily. But her primary feeling was of relief that she would no longer have to endure any more hurt provoked by Constantine's cruel comments. And she would protect herself from further heartache by staying as far away from him as possible.

'I think in view of what's just been said that we should try to avoid each other as much as possible while I'm still here,' she whispered.

Constantine's eyes narrowed. 'Are you *crazy*?' he questioned silkily, and without warning he splayed his hand over the sun-warmed expanse of her thigh, watching with triumph as her lips parted involuntarily in a soundless little gasp of pleasure. He lowered his voice. 'We may as well enjoy the one good, satisfactory thing which men and women *do* give each other. And—just for the record—I've done nothing but work in Athens; there have been no other women.' His black eyes gleamed with predatory anticipation. 'To be perfectly frank, your passion has left me unable to think of any other woman but you, *agape mou*.'

'And should I be flattered by that?' she questioned bitterly.

'I think perhaps you should,' he murmured.

But Laura was already scrambling to her feet and packing up the picnic basket.

'Oh, and Laura?' he said softly.

She looked up, some new steely quality in his voice warning her that what he was about to say would be more than another remark about their sexual chemistry. 'What?'

'I think it's about time we told Alex who I really am, don't you?'

Laura bit her lip. She had known this would happen, and it was happening sooner than she had hoped. But what was the point in delaying any more? Wouldn't that look as if they were hiding something shameful rather than giving them the opportunity to bond? Just because change was disrupting—and just because Laura was afraid of how telling Alex might affect their lives—it didn't mean that she could keep putting it off because it suited *her.*

'And your father?' she said softly. 'He'll need to know, too. Alex shouldn't be expected to keep the news to himself.'

In the end, the moment for telling Alex came quite naturally later that afternoon, when the three of them were sitting in the main town square of Livinos. Alex was eating ice-cream—an elaborate concoction of lemon and chocolate curls—and it seemed that every island resident stopped to ruffle his dark curls as they passed by.

'Why does everyone keep patting my head?' he questioned, not unhappily. 'And what do they keep saying to you?'

'By and large, the Greek people love having children around,' said Constantine, and Laura felt her heart lurch as she thought about his own mother. *But he's told you quite emphatically that he doesn't want your sympathy*, she reminded herself.

'Some of the older ones say that you look very much as I did at the same age,' added Constantine carefully.

'Do I?'

There was a pause. 'Very much so,' said Constantine gruffly, and then he looked across the table at Laura. She nodded. 'Do you have any idea why that might be?'

To Laura's surprise, Alex didn't answer straight away—just glanced from Constantine, to her, and then back to Constantine again. His dark eyes fixed on his father's face, a look of hope and longing tightening his boyish little features.

'Are you my daddy?' he asked.

Had it been the spoonful of ice-cream Alex had insisted on giving him which had caused this damned lump in his throat, making him momentarily incapable of words? Constantine swallowed. 'Yes, I am,' he said eventually.

There was no Hollywood movie scene of the son flinging himself onto his father's lap—that would have been too much in the circumstances. As they began to walk back towards the villa, Laura noticed Alex's fingers creep up towards the hand of the man by his side. And that Constantine took his son's little hand and was clasping it firmly, while looking fixedly ahead and blinking furiously, as if some piece of grit had just flown into his eye.

That evening, Constantine—with Laura standing nervously by his side—told his father that the Karantinos family did indeed have an heir, and that he had a grandson.

The old man stared at his son for a long moment and then gave a short laugh. 'You think I haven't already guessed that?' he questioned quietly. 'That you could bring a young child into this house out of the blue, with some flimsy excuse about him and his mother needing a holiday, a child who is the mirror-image of you at the same age, and that I would not realise that he was yours?'

Laura tried not to stare as she felt emotion build up like a gathering storm. She saw the old man take one tentative step forward, and silently willed the two men to embrace—to try to wipe out some of the heartache and bitterness which had built up between them. But Constantine took a corresponding step backwards—a step so subtle that many people would not have noticed. But Laura noticed. *Damn you, Constantine*, she thought furiously. *Damn you and your hard and unforgiving soul.* And his father noticed, too—for the lined face momentarily crumpled before he turned to look at her and nodded.

'You have a fine child in Alex, my dear. A happy and contented son for you to be proud of.'

'Th-thank you,' said Laura tremulously. 'It may seem odd to you that we kept it secret, but—'

Kyrios Karantinos shook his head. 'I can understand that circumstances may have been difficult,' he said gently. 'For I am not a complete ogre.' This was accompanied by a mocking glance at the silent figure of Constantine. 'Far better to approach things cautiously than to dive in. And Alex—he is happy to learn of the news?'

'He's ecstatic,' said Laura truthfully. As far as Alex was concerned it was *Constantine this* and *Constantine that*. Constantine had quickly become the centre of the impressionable young boy's universe. She'd watched the relationship developing between them and seen how badly her boy wanted a father—a man as a role-model. And Constantine never showed his fierce side with Alex, realised Laura.

'We must have a party to celebrate!' announced Kyrios

Karantinos suddenly. 'We could invite some people over from the mainland. It's a long time since we've thrown a big party.'

And, to Laura's surprise, Constantine nodded.

'Why not?' he questioned, with a shrug of his broad shoulders.

Laura turned away before either of them noticed the conflict of emotions she suspected were criss-crossing over her face, knowing that it was wrong to feel scared— but she did.

Despite their differences, the two proud men were gearing themselves up to announce to the world that the Karantinos family now had an heir—and the importance of such an heir to such a family could not be over-estimated. But aside from the bloodline issue there was something else which was just as important…and deep-down Laura hoped that Constantine and his father might be making the first steps towards a true reconciliation.

But where did that leave her? And Alex? She wanted him to forge a close relationship with both his father and his grandfather—of course she did. It was just the future which worried her now. Because how on earth were they going to handle it when she took Alex back to England at the end of the holidays? When he left sunshine and luxury behind him and returned to an old life which was looking greyer by the minute?

CHAPTER ELEVEN

'WHAT the hell are you doing?' demanded Constantine as he walked into the kitchen.

'What does it look like?' questioned Laura steadily, finding herself in the awkward situation of having to pretend to be normal and pleasant to Constantine in a situation which defied definition—made doubly difficult by the fact that she had been writhing passionately underneath the man in question in the early hours of that very morning. Pushing the erotic memory from her mind, she positioned another olive on one of the little feta tartlets, wanting to look at something—anything—other than the mocking distraction of his black eyes.

'Laura, put the damned dish down and look at me!'

Laura complied—knowing that if she didn't want to create discord then she didn't really have a lot of choice. 'What is it?'

'Why…?' He drew a deep breath. 'Why are you helping out in the kitchen?'

'Because we both agreed that would be my role here.'

'No, Laura,' he said heavily. '*You* insisted on it and *I* was railroaded into agreeing.'

'That must have been a first,' she said gravely.

Unwillingly, his mouth twitched. 'Very probably,' he agreed, before the sight of her beautiful body in that hideous-looking floral pinafore made the smile die instantly. 'I don't want you doing any more of this kind of work in the house and neither does my father. It is no longer appropriate. You are Alex's mother—and at the party tonight you will be introduced to the people of Livinos as such, not serving damned pastries to the guests!'

'But won't…?' She could feel her heart racing with nerves. How would the Karantinos family's friends and neighbours accept her—a pale little English waitress—as the mother of the Karantinos heir?

'Won't what?'

'Won't people think it strange? I mean, it's a small island. Everyone's going to want to know why I've been working here and now suddenly I've been revealed as the mystery mother. Why, even Demetra's been dying to ask, but she's so loyal to you and your father that she wouldn't dare.'

'I do not *care* what other people think,' he iced back. 'It is what *I* think that matters.'

'If you knew just how arrogant that sounded—'

His black eyes glittered. 'You didn't seem to be complaining about my arrogance when I ordered you to strip for me last night, *agape mou*. In fact, you told me that you had never been so turned on in your life.'

Laura flushed. Well, no—but characteristics which worked well within the bedroom did not always work in everyday life. 'Oh, very well,' she said quickly, in an effort to change the subject. 'I'll come to the party—if you insist.'

Fleetingly, it struck him as ironic that she—of all people—should sound as if she were conferring upon him a favour, when just about every other female of his acquaintance would have bitten his hand off for an invitation to what would be an undeniably glittering event.

'You will, of course, need something to wear.'

Laura felt her body stiffen with tension. 'What's the matter with the clothes I brought with me?' she questioned defensively. 'Too small-town and humble for the Karantinos family? Is that it?'

'Frankly, yes,' he drawled, his eyes mocking her as she took an angry step towards him. '*Ne*, just try it,' he murmured. 'Go on, Laura. Jab an angry finger at my chest and we both know what will happen. Except that it won't, because we can't—since Alex is having a chess lesson with my father just along the hall and Demetra is getting half the women in the village to bake bread for her. That is why I'm not able to ravish you here in the kitchen, or by the pool—or anywhere else for that matter.' He paused and he gave the flicker of a smile. 'So maybe you'll lose that indignation when I tell you about the dresses I've bought for you.'

Laura stared at him. 'You've…bought me *dresses*?'

He nodded as he met her uncomprehending look with one of his own. *Didn't* all *women like to be bought beautiful dresses?* he wondered. In his experience, the more money you lavished on a female, the more she adored you for it. 'When I was in Athens I took the opportunity to pick some up. You see, I knew that this kind of situation was bound to arise at some time, and that you'd need to look the part of a Karantinos woman.'

Her heart raced with anger and shame and hurt. Look the *part*? Because she was playing a role instead of being the real thing? Of course she was—or that would be how Constantine saw it.

The arrogant swine! He had bought her finery with his millions so that she would blend in, had he? Well, for once in her life—she would make sure she did the exact opposite and stand out at his wretched party!

'How very kind of you,' she said, mock-demurely, and saw him frown. 'I'll go and look at them.'

'No. Not now,' he said softly, and caught her wrist, bringing it up to his lips and whispering them against the fine tracery of veins which clothed the thready hammering of her pulse.

Just that brief touch weakened her, and Laura swayed and closed her eyes. 'Don't,' she whispered. 'You've just said yourself that the house is full of people.'

'Which is why we're going for a drive.'

Laura swallowed. 'Alex—'

'Is fine with my father. I've checked. Now, take off that damned pinafore and let's get going.'

Minutes later they were zipping their way along an isolated coastal road in a little silver sports car she hadn't seen before. 'Where exactly,' she questioned, 'are we going?'

'You'll see.'

The wind whipped through her hair and Laura felt ridiculously light-hearted. 'Suddenly you're an international man of mystery?'

'If that's what you'd like me to be,' he declared evenly, but her bright mood had affected him too, and he smiled.

Their destination turned out to be a beautiful stone house set back from the beach—but its simple beauty went unnoticed because they were barely inside the door before Constantine started kissing her and tugging at the zip of her dress.

'Aren't you going to…show me around?' she gasped.

'Aren't you?' he countered, and then closed his eyes as his fingers found her soft breasts. 'Come on, Laura. Show me around your body, *oreos mou*, show me deep inside your body—for that is the only place I want to go right now.'

His erotic words only spurred on Laura's own frantic desire. Half-clothed, they sank onto the marble floor—its cool surface contrasting perfectly with his hot flesh as it covered hers, their gasps morphing into ecstatic shuddered cries which split the silence.

Afterwards, they lay there—both with a fine dew of sweat drying on their skin—and Constantine stroked the mass of blonde hair which clouded her shoulders.

'Hot?'

'Boiling.'

'Fancy a swim?' he questioned idly.

Lazily, she stirred against his body, and yawned. 'I didn't bring a costume.'

Regarding her discarded panties, he splayed his hand possessively over one bare, warm globe of her bottom. 'Who says you'll need one? You can swim naked, my beauty.'

'Providing fodder for any passing voyeurs?' she said primly, even though she shivered beneath his touch and at the blatantly untrue compliment which had sprung from his lips.

Constantine laughed. 'It's utterly private and we won't be observed by a soul,' he said softly. 'That's why I brought us here. To see your body by daylight—for I am tired of having to be furtive. Of having to sneak into your room at night as if we are committing some sort of crime. I want the freedom to cry out when I come, and to watch while you do, too. To watch you walk around unfettered. I want to have sex with you in the sea, Laura,' he said thickly.

'*Oreos mou*, I want to have sex with you all day long—until our bodies are exhausted and our appetites sated.'

It wasn't the most romantic declaration she had ever heard, but it echoed Laura's own haunting desire for him. With her body she could show him her passion, even if her heart and her lips were prevented from giving voice to it. You could love a man with your lips in a different way than using them to tell him, she thought. And Constantine was right—the freedom to behave without constraint was completely intoxicating...

The afternoon sun was still bright when they drove back. Laura tried to tell herself that they were too exhausted for much conversation, but it was more than that. Her head was full of spinning thoughts.

Constantine had remained true to his vow that he was going to make love to her until they were both exhausted—she had never known that it was possible for desire to be ignited over and over again. He had made love to her on the beach, and then carried her down to the sea to wash the grains of sand from her skin. But the act of washing had awoken their sensual hunger once more—he had made her gasp and giggle until at last he had pulled her wet body against his and let the sea foam surge deliciously over their nakedness. Slippery and salty, she had let him part her legs beneath the water and felt their warm flesh join once more beneath the waves. And Constantine had been right—the freedom to make love without worrying about being overheard or seen was utterly intoxicating.

She thought about the party which lay ahead, and which until fairly recently would have terrified the life out of her. But that had been before this journey here to Livinos—a journey which had taught her as much about herself as about Greek life.

It had taught her that she loved the man who sat beside her, despite his cold heart which had been so damaged in his own childhood that it seemed to have no hope of healing. She loved him because he was Alex's father—but she suspected that she had loved him all those years ago, when she had given him her virginity so joyfully on that warm summer night. For wasn't love at first sight both the great dream and yet the admittedly rare reality of human relationships? Even if it hadn't been reciprocated it didn't mean it had necessarily gone away—and since she had become his lover that feeling had been growing as inexorably as a new shoot towards the spring sunshine. Hadn't the afternoon they'd just spent added to the magic?

She glanced at his hard and rugged profile as he stared at the coastal road ahead. The wind whipped through the black, tousled curls and the dark glasses shaded his eyes against the light—preventing her from reading anything of his own thoughts.

But who was she kidding? Those ebony eyes never gave anything away. And neither did he. He could buy her new dresses so that she wouldn't disgrace him at his fancy party—but he couldn't give her any of his heart or his soul even if he wanted to. He had locked those away a long time ago.

Back at the villa, they parted without a kiss or embrace—only the briefest of glittering looks from Constantine reminding her of how they'd spent the afternoon.

'I'll see you later,' he said softly, and resolutely turned his back on her before he was tempted to kiss her again.

Laura watched him go. Maybe for him it had just been an afternoon of amazing sex, she thought. He probably wasn't—like her—stupidly reliving every glorious second of it and pretending that it had anything to do with emotion.

It was with heightened colour that she went off to find Alex, who was now playing tennis with Stavros.

He waved his arm at her in greeting, and then adopted a fierce expression on his little face, wanting desperately to show his mother how good he'd become at the game.

How he'd grown to love sport, she thought tenderly. She stood by the side of the tennis court and watched as her son batted the ball over the net with what looked like incredible natural skill to her proud, motherly eye. Alex had been on a journey too, she recognised—he had realised some of his own dormant talents as well as getting to know his Greek family. And deep down she knew that nobody would ever dare bully him again. Laura watched as they changed ends, wondering once again how on earth he would ever be able to bear to leave this paradise of a place to go back to the very different life he knew in England.

She went to her room and showered off the sand, slipping into jeans and a T-shirt before surveying the garments Constantine had bought her, which someone had hung up in her wardrobe while she'd been out at the beach house. And although she'd told herself that she wasn't going to swoon over a few expensive articles of clothing she found herself doing just that.

Finest silk, cashmere and organza were here—represented in gowns which unbelievably fitted her like a glove. She twirled in front of the mirror in a vivid emerald silk. Though maybe it wasn't unbelievable at all—for wasn't Constantine one of those men who seemed to instinctively know more about a woman's body than she did?

But Laura didn't have a clue about dressing up. She'd never had the time, the money or the opportunity before—and suddenly she found herself longing for advice. Surely she could phone Sarah? She hadn't spoken to her sister for ages, and she missed her. With her artistic streak, Sarah had a brilliant eye and knowledge of clothes—she'd know which of these dresses would be most suitable.

She walked through the house, looking for Constantine, but he was nowhere to be found—only Kyrios Karantinos was in his study, sitting hunched over a book. He looked up as she tapped on the door.

'Looking forward to the party?' he questioned with a smile.

Laura wondered what he'd say if he had any idea of the confused emotions which were swirling around inside her. 'I'm not quite sure what to wear,' she admitted. 'And I wondered if it would be okay to use the telephone to ring my sister in England?' She hesitated, but then thought of the Karantinos billions and her own modest income. 'I've…I've got a cellphone, but it's…'

The old man gave a small smile as he gestured towards the telephone on the desk and began to get up. 'Please— say no more and come in. You must feel free to use the phone whenever you like, my dear.' His smile became a little wider. 'It is quite clear to me that Constantine has not ended up with a materialistic woman!'

She wanted to tell him that Constantine had not 'ended up' with this woman at all. 'Thank you—but I can go somewhere else to make the call. I don't want to push you out of your own study.'

'I was leaving shortly anyway.' He looked at her. 'I've been wondering what your future plans are?' he questioned, his faded eyes narrowing. 'Or maybe I shouldn't ask?'

Laura hesitated, knowing that she should not confide in Constantine's father—for mightn't Constantine see that as some kind of betrayal? 'No arrangements have been made yet,' she said uncertainly.

'You're good for him,' the old man said suddenly.

'No—'

'*Yes*. Better than anyone else has ever been for him.' A ragged sigh left his lips, as if it had been waiting for a long time to escape, and the old man looked at her with pain in his faded eyes. 'Better than I or his mother ever were, that's for sure.'

'I don't think—'

'I was a *bad* father—a very bad father,' interrupted Kyrios Karantinos fervently. 'I know that. I worshipped his mother—I was one of those foolish men who become obsessed by a woman. She dazzled me with her beauty and her youth so that I couldn't see anything but her.' There was a pause. 'And that kind of love is dangerous. It is blind. It meant that I could not tell the difference between fantasy and reality—and somewhere along the way was a very small and confused boy, cut adrift by the very two people who should have been looking out for him.' He gave a shuddering sigh. 'We both neglected him.'

How her heart ached for that little boy. 'Have you…have you tried to explain all this to Constantine?' she ventured cautiously. 'Tried to tell him how it was? I mean, how… how *sorry* you are now?'

'Oh, maybe a million times,' he admitted. 'But my proud and successful son will only hear what he wants to hear, and he finds the past too painful to revisit. Forgive me, Laura—for I do not mean to speak ill of him. You see…I love him.' His voice trembled. 'And I am an old man.'

She stared at him, suddenly understanding the subtext which lay behind his words. Soon he might die. And then the painful past might never be resolved—instead spreading its poisonous tentacles far into the future.

Briefly, he squeezed her arm and then left the study, and Laura stared out of the window at the beautiful Greek day, her heart almost breaking as she thought about the terrible distance between the two men which might never be bridged.

But she was here with a purpose. And—even if her worries about what to wear seemed rather flippant in comparison to what Kyrios Karantinos had just told her—she gathered together her troubled thoughts before dialling England.

It was strange speaking to her sister—it felt as if a lifetime had passed since they had last spoken—and Sarah was sounding very bubbly. 'The girl Constantine hired to work in the shop is *lovely*!' she enthused, and her voice dipped mischievously. 'And she has this *cousin*…he's called Matthius and he's just *gorgeous*!'

Aware of the rapidly spiralling cost of the call, Laura butted in. 'Sarah, I need your advice about clothes…'

Once Sarah had been given a brief run-down on all the dresses in the picture, she was emphatic. Laura must wear her hair up—'because sometimes when you wash it it goes into a cloud, and you end up looking like Alice in Wonderland.' And she should opt for the most fitted dress—'because what's the point of having a great figure if you can't show it off?'

That evening, Laura's hands were trembling as she swept an extra layer of mascara onto her lashes. She couldn't ever remember feeling this nervous before a party before—but maybe that wasn't so surprising. She'd overseen Alex getting dressed—Constantine had ensured that his son would be suitably kitted-out, too—and her heart had swelled with pride when she saw her little boy in a pair of long, dark trousers and a white shirt and little bow-tie. He looked so *Greek*, she thought.

But he is Greek. Or at least half-Greek.

Suddenly filled with fear, she stood in front of the mirror, but her head was so buzzing with disquiet that for a moment she did not see the image which reflected back at her. *Alex isn't going to want to leave this place*, she realised with a sinking heart. And could she really blame him?

Her eyes focussed on the mirror at last, and Laura blinked because for a moment it felt as if she was looking at a complete stranger. A sleek and sophisticated stranger with a costly dress and big, dark eyes?

There was a tap at the door and she turned round to see it opening. Constantine was standing there—his dark expression completely unreadable as he looked her up and down.

Nervously, Laura swallowed. 'Do you...do you like it?'

'I'm not sure,' he drawled.

'But you bought it! You're the one who wanted me to wear something grand.'

'*Ne.* I know I did,' he said slowly. He just had not been expecting such a complete...*transformation.* On the model in the showroom—who had flirted with him quite outrageously until his stony indifference had caused her to stop—the dress had looked completely different. But the blue satin moulded Laura's curves so closely that it looked as though she had been dipped in a summer sky. Above the low-cut bodice her skin glowed softly golden, and the curve of her breasts was a perfect swell. Her fine blonde hair was piled high on her head, with just a couple of recalcitrant locks tumbling down by the side of her face like liquid gold.

And her face! She rarely wore much make-up—sometimes nothing and she always looked as sexy as hell—but tonight the unaccustomed darkening of her eyes and the slick of gloss to her lips made her look like a siren. Every man would look at her and want her, thought Constantine— and a nerve flickered furiously at his temple.

'Do you like it?' repeated Laura, half tempted to tear the damned thing off and put on the little floral dress she'd brought with her from England.

'You look very *beautiful*,' said Constantine carefully. Putting his hand in his pocket, he withdrew a slim leather case. 'You'd better have these.'

'What are they?'

He flipped the lid open to reveal a bright scattering of ice-white jewels, and it took Laura's disbelieving eyes a couple of seconds to realise that she was in fact looking at a diamond necklace and a pair of long, glittering earrings.

'I can't wear these,' she breathed.

'Why not?'

'What if I lose one?'

'Don't worry—they're insured,' he said carelessly as he clipped the exquisite necklace around her neck. 'Put on the earrings, Laura.'

With trembling fingers she complied, and the piled up hairstyle complemented the waterfall earrings brilliantly as she stood before him for his assessment.

'Perfect,' he said softly. 'Now you look like a Karantinos woman.'

But as they walked out together towards the strings of lights which were already twinkling against the darkening sky Laura felt like a prize pony in a show, decked out with unfamiliar ribbons and with its mane plaited.

She was an impostor, she thought. A fraud. Externally

she carried all the displays of wealth which would be expected of the mother of Constantine's son. But inside? Inside she felt like a cork from a bottle which was lost on a vast and tossing ocean.

The party had all the elements for a successful evening, and the guests were determined to enjoy the fabled Karantinos hospitality. The weather was perfect, the finest wines flowed, and the village women had outdone themselves with the food. But part of Laura wished that she could hide behind the anonymity of her waitress's uniform instead of being subjected to the curious looks of the women of Livinos and—even more intimidating—of the society beauties who had flown in from Athens. They seemed to have no qualms about failing to hide their surprise when they were introduced to Laura. And neither did they abstain from flirting with Constantine.

Maybe she couldn't blame them, for he drew the eye irresistibly; no other man came even close to him. His hair looked ebony-black when contrasted against the snowy whiteness of his dinner jacket, which emphasised his powerful physique. And Alex stayed close by his side as Laura heard him being introduced over and over again as 'my son'.

My son, too she thought bitterly, ashamed of the great flood of primitive jealousy and fear which washed over her.

Because one look around at all the good and the great gathered here tonight was enough to ram home the extent of Constantine's power and influence. And not just here in his native Greece. Why, a world-famous architect had flown in from New York especially for this party!

But Laura knew how to behave. She knew that people couldn't tell how you were feeling if you disguised your nerves and concerns behind a bright party smile. It must be working too, because several of the men went out of their way to be charming to her.

The toast—to health and happiness and the continuation of the Karantinos bloodline—was taken early, so that Kyrios Karantinos could retire. He looked exhausted, thought Laura—and she accompanied him back to the house, keen to see he got there safely as well as enjoying a break from the sensation of being watched by the other guests.

She managed to get an excited Alex into bed before midnight, and by the time she had pulled the sheet over Blue Bear he was fast asleep. It was late, she reasoned. Too late to go back—and she was exhausted, too. All that endless smiling and trying not to sound like some gauche little woman who had shoe-horned her way into the life of the Greek billionaire by getting pregnant had completely wiped her out.

She showered and slipped into bed—half hoping that Constantine would not come to her tonight and half praying that he would. Couldn't she lose this terrible sense of insecurity in the warm haven of his arms? Forget life and all its problems in the dreamy pleasure of his lovemaking? Even if those feelings came crowding back in the moment he left.

The door opened and Constantine stood there unmoving—still in his dinner suit—just staring at the bed in silence before walking into the room and quietly shutting the door behind him.

'H-hello,' she said, sitting up and feeling rather stupid—why hadn't he come over to pull her hungrily into his arms?

'Can you get up and put some kind of robe on?' he asked, in a strained and distant kind of voice.

'Sure.' She looked up at him for some kind of hint as to what this was all about—but then she wished she hadn't.

Because it was like a cruel flashback to all those years ago
when she had looked into his eyes and seen nothing.

Nothing at all.

CHAPTER TWELVE

'Is…IS something wrong?' asked Laura tentatively.

Constantine turned round. The silky gown came to mid-thigh, and covered her in all the right places—but it did nothing to disguise the luscious curves and he did not want to be distracted by her body. Not yet.

'Nothing is wrong,' he said coolly. 'Why don't you sit down?'

He indicated the long window seat, which was scattered with squashy embroidered cushions, and Laura sank down onto it, wondering why he was talking to her in that strange tone. And why he hadn't kissed her. 'Why are you acting like this?' she asked, bewildered.

'I'm not *acting* like anything,' he ground out. 'I'm just wondering why you ran back to your room without saying goodnight to any of our guests?'

'Because they weren't *my* guests, they were *yours*!' she returned. 'They weren't here to see me, but you—and your father—and your son. I only had curiosity value as the woman who had given birth to him. Once they had seen me, I was superfluous to requirements.'

'Not to some of the male guests, you weren't!' he snarled. 'They could hardly stop undressing you with their eyes!'

'Well, you have only yourself to blame for that, Constantine,' she hissed back. 'Since you're the one who bought me the dress!'

'And I don't know why I did!'

'Oh, yes, you do,' she contradicted hotly. 'Because I just wasn't good enough, looking the way I normally look. You were afraid that I'd show you up!'

'I didn't want you to feel awkward.'

'You don't think I felt *awkward* with half a million pounds worth of diamonds strung around my neck?' She glanced over at the leather box. 'And can you please take them away with you? Just having them in the room makes me nervous.'

'Laura, why are you being like this?' he exploded.

Why, indeed? Because he made her feel cheap? As if the real Laura could only be tolerated if she was dressed up to look like someone else? *Because he would never love her as she wanted to be loved?* She raked her loose hair away from her face and looked at him in the bright moonlight which flooded in from the unshuttered windows.

'Being like *what*? *You're* the one who's burst in here with a face like ice!' she returned. 'So have you come here for something specific? Because I'm tired and I'd like to get to sleep.'

His eyes narrowed—it was the first time she had not melted automatically into his arms, eager for the closeness of his body.

'Yes, I came here for something specific,' he said, and his mouth hardened as he bit the words out. 'To ask you once again to marry me.'

It was ironic, thought Laura fleetingly, how something which you had only ever pictured in your wildest dreams should dissolve when it happened in real life. This was different from the last time he'd asked her—when they'd barely known each other. Because now they did. Now they were lovers who had shared time with one another—so that him asking her to marry him could be given proper consideration.

A proposal of marriage from the man she loved—supposedly the one thing her aching heart longed for. And yet it had been delivered with all the warmth of a giant chunk of ice floating in an Arctic sea.

She drew in a deep breath. 'Presumably to legitimise your son?'

He looked at her. Hadn't they been through too much for him to dress up the truth with niceties? He shrugged. 'Of course.'

Laura could have wept—or hurled the nearest object at his hard-hearted head. But since that happened to be the diamond set she didn't dare risk it.

He sensed her displeasure. 'Of course there would be more to our marriage than that.'

'There would?' she questioned hopefully.

He nodded. 'We have shown that we can live compatibly, *ne*?' His voice softened into a tone of pure silk. 'And in bed—or out of it—we are pure dynamite together, *agape mou*. You know that.'

Yes, she knew that—but wasn't that the most frightening thing of all? To have physical chemistry up there as one of the main reasons for being together. Because didn't everyone say that it faded in time? And then what would they be left with? A cold shell of a marriage. Already she could imagine the reality of such a marriage, and an icy chill made her begin to shiver, despite the heavy warmth of the night.

'No,' she said.

'No?' His voice was incredulous, and he took a step forward. 'How can you say no when you know that it is what Alex would want,' he said, his voice dangerously soft. 'What Alex *wants*.'

Her fingers flew to her throat and she stared at him in fear. 'Have you asked him? Gone behind my back to get him to side with you?' she demanded hoarsely.

His mouth twisted. 'You think me capable of such an act, Laura? No, I have not—but you know that what I say is true. The boy loves it here—you have only to look at him to see how much he has blossomed since he arrived.'

Guilt shafted through her heart. Hadn't she thought the very same herself—and had he guessed that? 'But that's... *blackmail*,' she whispered.

No. It was fighting for what was truly his—something which he had discovered meant more to him than all his properties and ships and the international acclaim he enjoyed. His son meant far more to him than the continuation of a bloodline...young Alex had crept into his heart and found a permanent home there. Was Laura prepared to ride roughshod over their son's wishes purely for her own ends?

'Ask him,' he taunted. 'Go on—ask him!'

But Constantine's cruel words focussed Laura's mind on what really mattered, and now she got up and faced him, staring mulishly up at him. It was true that he towered over her, and made her feel ridiculously small, but she didn't care. She might be small but she certainly wasn't insignificant. And he *would* hear her out!

'No, I *won't* ask him—because I wouldn't marry you if you were the last man on earth!' she hissed. 'A man so cruel and so cold that he can't bear to forgive his own father.

Even though that father has asked him time and time again to forgive him for all the wrongs he admits he did!'

'Have you been speaking with my father?' he demanded furiously.

'And what if I have? Is that such a heinous crime?' she retorted. 'Am I supposed to ask your permission if I want to speak to somebody?'

'You dare to accuse me of going behind *your* back, and now I discover that you have done exactly the same!' he thundered.

'Oh, please don't try and get out of it by using logic!' she flared, showing a complete lack of it herself. 'Your father made mistakes, yes—and so did your mother. Though it sounds to me as if she couldn't help her own behaviour, and some people are like that. Weak. Unable to give love—even to their own children. And *they can't help it*, Constantine—they were born that way!'

He clenched his fists in fury. How dared she? How *dared* she? 'Have you quite finished?'

That intimidating tone would have silenced many people, but Laura was too passionate to stop. This meant far too much for her to be able to stop. 'No, I have *not* finished! I can't believe you even made the suggestion that I marry you. You're still angry about the coldness of your own childhood and yet you want to subject Alex to more of the same!'

'What the hell are you talking about, Laura?'

This was painful; maybe too painful—and Laura was not prepared to go as far as admitting that if they married then the balance of love would be as one-sided as in his parents' own marriage. Because he didn't realise she loved him, did he? And wouldn't it give him power over her if he did?

'I'm talking about bringing a child up within a loveless marriage—it's just not fair. Things would only get worse between us—never better—and as Alex grew he would have to tiptoe around our feelings and our animosities. What kind of example is that to set him?' she said, her voice beginning to tremble as she thought of her darling son. 'What hope is there for him to be happy in his own life if he looks around and sees discord all around him? How can he believe in love and happiness for himself if he never sees an example of it at home, Constantine?'

Her breath had deserted her and her words died away. She had nothing left to say—but she did not think she needed to. For Constantine's face had suddenly become shuttered. And his eyes—always enigmatic—now looked like strange, cold stones. As if a light had gone out behind them.

'This is what you think?' he demanded.

'Yes,' she whispered, although it broke her heart to admit it. 'Because it's the truth.'

For a moment there was silence—a heavy and uncomfortable kind of silence—and then Constantine's mouth hardened.

'Very well, Laura,' he said, in a voice of pure steel. 'I can see the sense behind your words, since they are—as you say—the truth. And at least if you go then I will no longer have to endure your intolerable interference in things which do not concern you.'

She prayed her lips would not crumple, nor her eyes give her pain away. 'Constantine—'

But he silenced her with his next statement. 'We will need to make plans. And we must do it so that everyone benefits as far as possible. You will require financial assistance. *No*!' He held his hand up peremptorily, anticipating her objections. A harsh note of bitterness entered his voice. 'This is not the time for pretty displays of unnecessary pride,' he spat out. 'You are the mother of my son and I insist that you have an adequate income to support him in a manner which I hope we can both agree on. I want him to go to a school where he isn't bullied—'

'Who told you that?'

'He did, of course,' he said impatiently. 'Not in so many words—but it was clear to me that he is not as happy as he could be. He needs a school where there is plenty of sport, and you need enough money to take that haunted look out of your eyes, never to have to supplement your income with damned waitressing jobs again. And I…' He drew a deep breath as pain like he had never known rushed in to invade the heart he had tried to protect for so long. 'I want to see as much of Alex as possible—we'll need to come to some agreement on that.'

She wanted to reach out to him. To tell him that he could see as much of Alex as he wanted—to reassure him and to comfort him that they would do the best they possibly could. But there was something so icy and forbidding about his words and demeanour that she did not dare. Suddenly he had become a stranger to her. 'Of course,' she said stiffly.

'I will arrange for you to return to England as soon as possible. I think that best, in the circumstances. My lawyers will be in touch on your return. But I want some time alone with Alex tomorrow morning.' He drew a deep breath as reality hit him, seeming to turn his whole body into stone. He forced the next words out. 'To say goodbye to my son.'

CHAPTER THIRTEEN

'BUT Mum, *why* do we have to go home?'

Laura's smile didn't slip, even though her face felt as if it had been carved out of marble—but during the sleepless night which had followed her furious row with Constantine she had decided the best way to handle questions like this. And the best way was to present her and Alex leaving Livinos as something perfectly normal. *Which it was.*

'Well, we only ever planned to come out for a few weeks,' she reminded him. 'Remember?'

'It's been less than that,' said Alex sulkily. 'And I like it here.'

She knew that—and it broke her heart to have to drag him away—but what choice did she have? He'd been happy in England before and he would be happy again—especially if there was no more bullying and if he changed schools, as Constantine himself had suggested. And didn't all the books on child rearing say that the worst thing you could do was to subject your children to a hostile atmosphere and infighting between parents? She could do worse than remind herself of the bitter words she and Constantine had exchanged last night if she needed any more convincing that the two of them were basically incompatible.

'Anyway,' said Laura, with a brightly cheerful smile, even though the thought of the future terrified her, 'you'll be coming back to Livinos lots…to see your daddy. And he'll be coming to England to take you out. You'll…well, you'll have the best of both worlds, really, Alex!'

Alex bit his lip, as if he couldn't bring himself to agree with this. 'Can I go swimming with Stavros, please?'

Laura felt her heart threaten to break as she saw his pinched little face. 'Of course you can,' she whispered. 'But you've only got a couple of hours. The helicopter will be leaving straight after lunch, and we mustn't be late.'

He didn't say another word as she took him outside to find the affable Greek student, and Laura stood there, watching the two of them heading towards the pool area, her eyes full of rogue tears which she fiercely blinked back.

Returning to her room, she finished packing—folding her cheap clothes into neat piles and then stuffing them into the equally cheap suitcase. For a brief moment her fingers strayed towards the costly gowns Constantine had bought her, and then strayed back again. Because what was the point of taking them back to England? They had been purchased with the sole purpose of making her look like a Karantinos woman—and she wasn't one and never would be. She had no right to wear the exquisite garments and they had no place in her life—where on earth could she possibly wear them in Milmouth?

Packing up Alex's stuff was harder—because here she really was tempted to take some of the wonderful toys and books Constantine had provided for him. But even if they took a whole load back—where on earth would they find room to accommodate them in their tiny apartment? And besides, they would always be here for him when he visited.

Laura swallowed the sudden acrid taste of fear. Because wasn't that an additional cause of her fretting heart? The fact that Alex would have his wonderful little world kept intact here—a world of toys and swimming pools, boats and planes, and the growing knowledge that he was heir to the fabulous Karantinos fortune...not simply the son of a struggling single mother. Would the day come when he chose to live out the Greek side of his heritage—rejecting her and the country of his birth?

Alex wouldn't *do* that, she told herself desperately—but still the fear ate away at her.

Their packing completed, Laura stole a glance at her watch. She had already said a brief and upsetting farewell to Constantine's father, and to Demetra, too. Goodbyes were awful at the best of times, but these felt a million times worse—loaded down with the terrible and aching significance of all that she was leaving behind. And most upsetting of all was the thought of leaving Constantine.

Was she being crazy? Wouldn't it make more sense if she gritted her teeth and accepted the fact that, while he didn't love her, Constantine would provide a secure childhood for Alex?

But not a *loving* childhood, she reminded herself. And she knew that this was about far more than her ego being bruised because Constantine didn't love *her*. Why, he couldn't even forgive his father. How could she let Alex exist in an emotionally cold world like that?

Laura glanced at her watch. The time was ticking away, and her stomach was churning with the kind of slow dread she got before an exam. What the hell was she going to do between now and the arrival of the helicopter, which would whisk them to Athens to catch the private jet which this time she had been unable to refuse? Maybe she would take one last lingering tour of the beautiful grounds which surrounded the Karantinos property.

Slipping out of the villa into the dappled sunlight, Laura thought how strange the atmosphere around the place seemed today. Was it because Constantine was nowhere to be seen? Or maybe it was just her.

She could hear the distant splash of Alex and Stavros larking around in the pool, and she could see a sleek white yacht down on the sapphire waters of the sea—but none of it seemed real. She felt as if she was insubstantial; a ghost of a woman who walked through the fruit orchards and tried to focus on the scent of the pine trees rather than the tearing ache in her heart.

Walking further across the property than she had ever ventured before, she came across a small bougainvillaea-tumbled grove. It was a scented, secret sort of place, reached through a dusty tract of olive trees and shaded from the glaring heat of the sun by tumbling blooms, and she sank down on a stone bench, wishing that she'd drunk some water before leaving the house.

For a while she sat there, trying to decide about what she would do when she got back to Milmouth. Maybe she'd think about selling more local produce in the shop—asking villagers if they wanted to shift any leftover crops from large gluts of home-grown vegetables. That would benefit everyone in the community, wouldn't it? But the question seemed to have no real relevance in her life. *Please help me to feel part of that community again,* she prayed. *And not like some sad woman who's left her heart and her soul behind in this paradise.*

'Hiding away, are you, Laura?'

A deep and familiar voice shattered the silence, and Laura's heart leapt as Constantine stepped into the grove— his hard face shuttered, the dappled light casting shadows over the high slash of his cheekbones. She looked up into his eyes, but met nothing but cool curiosity in their ebony depths.

'Why would I be hiding?' she questioned, her voice sounding light in contrast to the hard thundering of her heart.

He shrugged as he sat down beside her. 'This isn't a place you usually frequent.'

'Then how did you know I was here?'

There was a pause. 'I followed you.'

Another pause. Longer this time. And now her heart was beating so hard and so fast that Laura could barely stumble the words out. 'Wh-why would you do that?'

His eyes rested on the lightly tanned length of her slender thighs, their shape clearly outlined by the thin cotton dress she wore. Why, indeed? Because she continued to mesmerise him—even though he had vowed not to let her? Constantine's mouth twisted as he felt the slow throb of blood to his pulse points. How many times had he told himself that she exerted an allure simply because she had refused him—because she had done the inexplicable and turned down his offer of marriage for a second time?

He met the wide grey eyes which were observing him so guardedly, and noted the fall of fine blonde hair which was hanging around her narrow shoulders like a pale cloud. Had she read one of those books which advised holding out in order to increase her worth as a woman? He felt the stab of desire jerking insistently at his groin. Well, she would learn soon enough that he would not be played with—not any more. She had had her chance and that chance would not return. But in the meantime he would have her one last time!

'Why, Constantine?' she persisted. 'Why did you follow me?'

He picked up her unresisting hand and studied it. 'Oh, I don't know.' Running the pad of this thumb questingly over the centre of her palm, he felt her shiver. 'Any ideas?'

Laura felt her already dry throat grow completely parched. His touch. His proximity. The sudden glint from his eyes. All those things were making her feel weak and helpless.

She told herself to pull her hand away. To move. To distract him.

So why did she stay exactly where she was? Letting Constantine stroke enchanting little circles over her skin and feeling herself tremble in response?

'Mmm, Laura?' he questioned, as he shifted his body a little closer on the bench. 'Any ideas?'

'N-no.'

'Really? How remarkably unimaginative of you, *agape mou*. Why, I'm quite disappointed that someone whom I have coached so tirelessly in the art of love shouldn't immediately take advantage of a sweet and final opportunity presenting itself like this.'

His words were in a muddle in her head. Dangerous words—of which *final* seemed to be the most dangerous of all. *You both know it's over*, she told herself desperately— *so why are you letting him pull you onto his lap? And why aren't you stopping him from sliding your panties right down, from putting his fingers between your legs and...*

'Constantine!' she gasped.

He kissed her to shut her up—but also because he wanted to kiss her. *Needed* to kiss her. To punish her and to make her hurt as he was hurting. But the kiss didn't stay that way—infuriatingly, it transformed itself into a terrible aching hunger which could be eased in only one way. He tore his mouth away and shuddered out a harsh entreaty.

'Undo my jeans.'

Laura didn't even hesitate before she tremblingly obeyed—indeed, she thought that she might have been scrabbling at his belt even before that terse instruction had been whispered in her ear.

She gasped again as she freed him—marvelling at the sheer power of him. He looked and felt so big and so erect in her tiny hand as she stroked on the condom he gave her. And then he began impatiently to tug at the jeans, until they had slithered down to his ankles. He didn't even bother to kick them off. Instead, he just lifted her up, as if she were made of cotton wool, bringing her down deep onto his aching shaft and kissing her again with a fierce hunger—sensing that her shuddering little cries of fulfilment were only minutes away. As were his. A few ecstatic movements of her hips and he was groaning into her mouth as he felt himself spasming against her own honeyed contractions.

Afterwards, she collapsed against him, burying her head on his shoulder, willing the tears not to come, and wondering why everything felt so confused. Why had he done this—and why had she let him? Registering that sex had a dark power which managed to distort what had seemed such a straightforward decision, she found herself wondering if she had been wrong to tell him she was leaving.

If he asks me again to stay, then I might just say yes, she thought weakly—but the next thing she knew was Constantine firmly lifting her off him.

'Straighten your clothes,' he said abruptly as he began

to pull up the zip of his jeans. He hated his weakness around her—the way he couldn't seem to resist her when every logical pore in his formidable body told him that it should be easy. Would she see this as another little triumph? he wondered bitterly. Another perfect demonstration of how she had the powerful Constantine Karantinos eating out of her hand?

'I'll leave you to find your own way back,' he finished, raking angry fingers back through the tousled waves of his black hair.

And then he was gone, and Laura could hardly believe what had just taken place. How she could have let him arrive and just...*do* that to her? But she *had* let him. More than let him—had squirmed with pleasure and enjoyed every erotic second of it—so if Constantine had now lost all respect for her as a woman then she had only herself to blame.

But in a way her orgasm had emptied her of all feeling and all emotion—and at least that made the last preparations for her departure bearable. So that she was able to chat excitedly to Alex about the conkers which would be on the autumn trees in England—ignoring the morose set of his little face in response. Only once did her composure threaten to buckle, and that was when Constantine clasped his son in a hug which went on and on.

Then he ruffled the little boy's dark curls and smiled. 'I'll come and see you soon in England,' he said.

Alex's crumpled face was turned upwards, as if he had just seen the first light in a dark sky. 'When?'

'How does next month sound?'

'Oh, it sounds wonderful, Papa.'

The helicopter blades whirred round and round, and Laura glanced out of the window to see Constantine staring up intently at his son. She felt a real pang of remorse. Was she doing a wrong and selfish thing by taking Alex back to England? Yet how many women would willingly trap themselves on an island this size with a man who didn't love them?

The island retreated as the craft took off, but Constantine stood there long after the black speck had grown smaller and smaller and then finally disappeared, his shoulders bowed with the weight of something too painful to analyse.

Something which made all the Karantinos billions fade into pale insignificance.

CHAPTER FOURTEEN

AS THE last of Alex's footsteps died away, Laura closed the front door and let out a long sigh of something which felt like relief. *Please let him have a nice day with my sister,* she prayed silently. *Please remove some of the inevitable disappointment which has clouded my son's face since returning home from Greece last week.* A week which had felt more like a year.

It was strange to be back in England, and even stranger to be back in their small flat which no longer seemed to feel like home. *And why was that?* she wondered guiltily. Because it was small and poky after the vast Karantinos villa? Or because the powerful presence of Constantine was absent—making the place seem soulless?

'I miss my papa,' Alex had told her on more than one occasion—in a way which tore at Laura's conscience.

And, so do I, she thought. *So do I.* A decision she had made for all the best reasons was now proving to be unbearable—and it seemed that she had no one in the world to turn to or confide in.

Because even Sarah seemed to have moved on. Her sister had been hurtling up to London at every opportunity to see Matthius—the cousin of the Greek student Constantine had roped in to help while Laura had been away. It seemed that like Demetra, Mattius was also a member of the Constantine Karantinos fan-club, having convinced Sarah that the billionaire was only arrogant and cold to the many people who wanted something from him—but that to friends and family he was loyalty personified.

For Laura, who was trying desperately hard to put the Greek tycoon from her mind, this was the last thing she wanted or needed to hear. Was it her stricken face which had made Sarah offer to take Alex out for the day? Or the fact that she couldn't seem to settle to anything and was driving everyone mad?

Whatever the reason, it was very kind of her sister, and Laura knew it was good for Alex to have something to occupy his thoughts other than the life he had left behind on Livinos. But the free day yawned emptily ahead of her, and Laura found herself wondering how she was going to fill the aching hours ahead when she heard a loud banging on the door. She ran back into the hall to throw it open with more than a little relief.

'Now what have you forgotten—?' she began to say, but the words died on her lips when she saw who was standing there. Not Alex. Nor Sarah. But…

Constantine?

Laura swallowed, shaking her head a little, blinking back the stupid sting of disbelieving tears as she stared up at him. She'd been thinking about him non-stop. Dreaming about him constantly. Her thoughts about him had driven her half mad and her heart had been unable to stop aching—so that for a moment it just felt like an extension of all her desires that he would somehow magically appear. As if the man who stood in front of her wasn't real. As if he couldn't be real.

But he was. Laura stared at the formidable physique of Constantine Karantinos—standing on her doorstep, with his dark hair all windswept and a look on his face she had never seen before. Had she forgotten just how gorgeous he was? How strong and how vital? How he could dominate a space simply by existing in it?

'Constantine,' she breathed, and her heart began to pound with frantic yearning. She wanted to touch him. To throw her arms around him. To whisper her fingertips wonderingly along the hard, proud line of his jaw—as if only touch alone would convince her that he was really here. 'Wh-what are you doing here?' she questioned.

It was then that she realised. Of course! He had come to see his son. Their heartbreaking farewell on the airstrip must have made him vow to come and see Alex earlier than he had intended. And even though she would have liked some warning that he was about to appear, so that she wouldn't have answered the door in a scruffy old pair of jeans and a T-shirt which had seen better days, she managed a brisk kind of smile.

Think of Alex, she told herself—he's the one who matters.

So she was able to look up at him with genuine regret. 'Oh, what a pity. Alex has just gone out.'

'I know he has.'

She looked at him blankly. 'You do?'

'Yes. I rang Sarah this morning and asked her if she would take him out for the day.'

'You rang Sarah?' she repeated. 'And she...*agreed*?'

'Yes, she did.'

Laura blinked at him in confusion. It was true that her sister no longer seemed to think that he was the devil incarnate—but agreeing to Constantine's request behind her back sounded awfully like *collusion*, and…and… Well, it threw up all kinds of questions. 'But *why*?' she whispered.

He raised his dark brows in sardonic query. 'Do you want me to tell you when I'm standing on the doorstep?'

Registering the faintly reprimanding tone of his question, she pulled the door open wider. 'No. No, of course not. Come in.' But as he passed her she had to clutch the door handle to balance herself—his very proximity was producing a terrible wave of weakness and longing which threatened to destabilise her.

He was standing in their cramped little hallway— making it look even smaller, if that were possible—and Laura shook her head uncomprehendingly. Because if he wasn't here to see Alex, then…then…

'Please tell me why you're here,' she said, her voice a whisper as thready as her erratic heartbeat.

His black gaze was calculating. 'No ideas at all, Laura?'

Numbly, she shook her head, and it was then that Constantine realised that there was no easy way to do this—or she wasn't going to make it easy for him—and maybe that was the way it should be. Maybe he too needed to experience doubt and uncertainty, as well as the fear that she might reject him again.

But words describing feelings didn't come easy when you'd spent a lifetime avoiding them—and for a moment he felt like a man who had found himself on a raft in the middle of the ocean, unsure of which direction to take. He sucked air into lungs which suddenly felt empty.

'I have thought about everything you said that last night. About love and about the past.' He saw the way she was staring at him, her pale face fierce, chewing on her bottom lip the way she always did when she was concentrating hard. 'And the impact of both those things on the present and the future.' There was a pause. 'They were things I didn't want to hear,' he whispered. 'Things I tried to block my ears to. But somehow—I couldn't do it. And when my anger had died away, I realised that you were right. That I needed to forgive my father—and in a way I needed to forgive my mother, too.'

'Constantine—'

'So that's what I've come to tell you. That I have. I have had a long talk with my father and told him…'

Momentarily his voice tailed away, and Laura lifted up her hand. 'You don't…have to tell me if you don't want to,' she whispered, seeing the pain of memory etched on his hard features and finding that it was hurting her, too.

'Oh, but that's where you're wrong. You see, I do, Laura. I need to tell you plenty of things—just as I did my father.' He sucked in another breath—because although Constantine was a brave man, opening up his heart to her like this took courage of a different kind. 'I told him that it was now time for us to be a true father and son to each other—and for him to be a grandfather to Alex.'

Laura nodded as his sudden appearance at last began to make sense. She guessed what was coming. He was going to ask her to take Alex back to Greece, to help facilitate his relationship with his father—a man too old and infirm to travel great distances. And, although it wasn't ideal, Laura knew she was going to say yes. It didn't matter if he wasn't offering her the dream ticket of love *with* marriage—she'd settle for whatever she could get. For everyone's sake. Because she'd had a chance to live the alternative—a life without Constantine—and that life was bleak. Like a vase which was permanently empty of flowers. And didn't she have more than enough love to go round—for all of them? Couldn't she perhaps show him *how* to love—with the hope that one day he might be able to give a little love back to her? Was it pathetic of her to be prepared to settle for that?

'That sounds perfect,' she agreed.

Constantine's eyes narrowed. 'Does it?' he questioned, and suddenly his voice sounded harsh. 'Not to me, it doesn't.'

And now a very real fear lanced through her. Perhaps he *wasn't* asking her to marry him at all—hadn't he already asked her twice and she'd turned him down? Would a proud man like this really ask her a third time? Why, she was probably being completely arrogant in not accepting that deep down he'd been delighted to see the back of her. 'Why not?' she breathed painfully.

He stared at her. The bare feet. The shapeless jeans— and a T-shirt which Demetra would probably have used to polish the tiles with. It was inconceivable that such a woman as Laura had captured his heart, but captured it she had—and so tightly that at this moment it was threatening to burst right out of his chest. Her physical ensnarement of him had never been in any doubt—but her purity and loyalty to him as a lover thrilled him to the very core of his being. As did her fierce determination to protect her son, and her admirable refusal to accept his offer of marriage, showing him that she was not a woman who could be bought by his colossal wealth.

'Because I have been a fool,' he declared hotly. 'I have failed to see what was right beneath my very nose—that you, Laura, are the woman who makes me laugh, who challenges me. The woman who is not afraid to tell me the truth. Who kisses more sweetly than I ever thought it possible to kiss. Who makes diamonds look dull and starlight seem mediocre.'

He drew a ragged breath, knowing that he had still not gone far enough—but admitting love for the first time in his life was hard for a man who had only ever seen warped examples of that emotion.

He stared at her, his heart pounding in his chest, aware as he looked at her that if he said it he had to mean it. *Really* mean it. And suddenly it was easy.

'You are the woman I love,' he said softly. 'I love you, Laura. I love you so much.'

'Oh, Constantine…' she breathed, scarcely able to believe what he was saying to her. But just one look at the incredible tension on his beautiful face told her that every word was true.

'But the question is do you love *me*?' he demanded.

Was he *crazy*? 'Yes—*yes*!'

'As fiercely as I do you?'

'Oh, yes!'

'Then for the third time of asking—and because I am finally running out of patience—will you please marry me, Laura?'

Her smile broke out, so wide it felt as if it would split her face in two. 'Yes! Oh, God, yes. I love you. I *love* you, Constantine! I've loved you for so long that I don't know any other way—but, oh, I can't tell you how wonderful it is to actually be able to say it out loud!'

'Promise me you'll never stop saying it,' he declared, amazed at his own need to hear it.

'Oh, I won't—my sweet, darling Constantine.'

He pulled her into his arms, and this time he really *did* destabilise her, for her knees gave way—but Constantine was holding onto her as tightly as could be as he began to kiss her. And this kiss was different from any other they had ever shared. It was tender and healing as well as passionate, and it sealed their love properly—ending all twists and turns along the way which had brought them here to this point.

And if it was a kiss which was mingled with their tears—then didn't that somehow make it sweeter and more precious still?

EPILOGUE

THE wedding took place in Greece—with Sarah as bridesmaid and Alex carrying two platinum rings on a little cushion. Knowing the sensibilities of young boys, Laura had told him that he didn't *have* to be involved in the ceremony, but Alex had insisted. He was so happy, Laura realised—blissfully contented that his mother and his father were going to be married at last.

It was a small ceremony, with a big party afterwards, and because it was held on the island it meant that the press could be kept largely in check. Unexpectedly, the message of congratulations which brought most satisfaction to bride and groom was sent by the supermodel formerly known as Ingrid Johansson, who was now Mrs Ingrid Rockefeller, and living in luxury in the centre of Manhattan. It read:

You did me a favour, *alskling*—I have now a man who adores me, and we were married last month.

Laura had long ago realised that Constantine had already finished with the supermodel when she had burst into his life again, but it gladdened her heart to know that the Swedish beauty was happy.

Sarah had landed herself a place at art school in London, and was planning a new life for herself there. So they'd sold their bakery shop and the flat for a very respectable sum which had gone towards buying her an apartment near her college. And Sarah—after a little persuasion—had allowed Laura and Constantine to pay off the balance of her new home.

'You've helped me for years,' Laura had told her fiercely. 'So please let me pay back something for all your time and kindness.'

It was decided that Alex would go to the school on Livinos until he was old enough to continue his studies on the mainland—just as his father had done. And, as well as taking an intensive course in Greek, Laura was planning to open a bakery on the island. Demetra had moaned about the lack of a bread shop often enough, and Laura recognised that she had a real gift for making a small business work. Two local women had been employed to help her, and if other babies came along—well, then Laura knew there were heaps of people she could call on.

But for now the shop gave her a role and a purpose on Livinos—it meant that she was more than just Constantine's new wife, and that was important to her. And, she suspected, to him. One of the reasons he had fallen in love with her—so he told her on their wedding night—was because she was so proud and independent. She was the only woman he'd ever known who hadn't coveted diamonds.

In fact, this lack of enthusiasm for fine jewels had proved to be the only problem in the blissfully problem-free time leading up to their wedding.

'It is traditional for the groom to give his beautiful bride a gift,' he murmured, pulling her into his arms and drifting his lips against hers. 'But—since diamonds don't impress you—what on earth can I give you as a wedding present that is equally precious, *agape mou*?'

And Laura smiled, because the question was superfluous. She already had the thing she most wanted—the most precious thing on this earth. The love of a man she adored.

Constantine's love.

* * * * *

Turn the page for an exclusive extract from
RAFFAELE: TAMING HIS TEMPESTUOUS VIRGIN
by
Sandra Marton

"In that case," Don Cordiano said, "I give my daughter's hand to my faithful second in command, Antonio Giglio."

At last, the woman's head came up. "No," she whispered. "No," she said again, and the cry grew, gained strength, until she was shrieking it. "No! No! No!"

Rafe stared at her. No wonder she'd sounded familiar. Those wide, violet eyes. The small, straight nose. The sculpted cheekbones, the lush, rosy mouth...

"Wait a minute," Rafe said, "just wait one damned minute...."

Chiara swung toward him. The American knew. Not that it mattered. She was trapped. Trapped! Giglio was an enormous blob of flesh; he had wet-looking red lips and his face was always sweaty. But it was his eyes that made her shudder, and he had taken to watching her with a boldness that was terrifying. She had to do something....

Desperate, she wrenched her hand from her father's.

"I will tell you the truth, Papa. You cannot give me to Giglio. You see—you see, the American and I have already met."

"You're damned right we have," Rafe said furiously.

"On the road coming here. Your daughter stepped out of the trees and—"

"I only meant to greet him. As a gesture of—of goodwill." She swallowed hard. Her eyes met Rafe's and a long-forgotten memory swept through him: being caught in a firefight in some miserable hellhole of a country when a terrified cat, eyes wild with fear, had suddenly, inexplicably run into the middle of it. "But—but he—he took advantage."

Rafe strode toward her. "Try telling your old man what really happened!"

"What *really* happened," she said in a shaky whisper, "is that…is that right there, in his car—right there, Papa, Signor Orsini tried to seduce me!"

Giglio cursed. Don Cordiano roared. Rafe would have said, "You're crazy, all of you," but Chiara Cordiano's dark lashes fluttered and she fainted, straight into his arms.

* * * * *

Be sure to look for
RAFFAELE: TAMING HIS TEMPESTUOUS VIRGIN
by Sandra Marton
available November 2009
from Harlequin Presents®!

Darkly handsome—proud and arrogant
The perfect Sicilian husbands!

RAFFAELE: TAMING HIS TEMPESTUOUS VIRGIN
by
Sandra Marton

The patriarch of a powerful Sicilian dynasty,
Cesare Orsini, has fallen ill, and he wants atonement
before he dies. One by one he sends for his sons—
he has a mission for each to help him clear his
conscience. But the tasks they undertake will
change their lives for ever!

Book #2869
Available November 2009

Pick up the next installment from Sandra Marton
DANTE: CLAIMING HIS SECRET LOVE-CHILD
December 2009

HPI2869

REQUEST YOUR FREE BOOKS!

 HARLEQUIN *Presents*®

 PASSION GUARANTEED SEDUCTION

2 FREE NOVELS PLUS 2 FREE GIFTS!

YES! Please send me 2 FREE Harlequin Presents® novels and my 2 FREE gifts (gifts are worth about $10). After receiving them, if I don't wish to receive any more books, I can return the shipping statement marked "cancel". If I don't cancel, I will receive 6 brand-new novels every month and be billed just $4.05 per book in the U.S. or $4.74 per book in Canada. That's a savings of close to 15% off the cover price! It's quite a bargain! Shipping and handling is just 50¢ per book*. I understand that accepting the 2 free books and gifts places me under no obligation to buy anything. I can always return a shipment and cancel at any time. Even if I never buy another book, the two free books and gifts are mine to keep forever.

106 HDN EYRQ   306 HDN EYR2

Name _____ (PLEASE PRINT)

Address _____ Apt. #

City _____ State/Prov. _____ Zip/Postal Code

Signature (if under 18, a parent or guardian must sign)

Mail to the **Harlequin Reader Service:**
IN U.S.A.: P.O. Box 1867, Buffalo, NY 14240-1867
IN CANADA: P.O. Box 609, Fort Erie, Ontario L2A 5X3

Not valid to current subscribers of Harlequin Presents books.

Are you a current subscriber of Harlequin Presents books and want to receive the larger-print edition? Call 1-800-873-8635 today!

* Terms and prices subject to change without notice. Prices do not include applicable taxes. Sales tax applicable in N.Y. Canadian residents will be charged applicable provincial taxes and GST. Offer not valid in Quebec. This offer is limited to one order per household. All orders subject to approval. Credit or debit balances in a customer's account(s) may be offset by any other outstanding balance owed by or to the customer. Please allow 4 to 6 weeks for delivery. Offer available while quantities last.

Your Privacy: Harlequin Books is committed to protecting your privacy. Our Privacy Policy is available online at www.eHarlequin.com or upon request from the Reader Service. From time to time we make our lists of customers available to reputable third parties who may have a product or service of interest to you. If you would prefer we not share your name and address, please check here. ☐

HP09R

EXTRA

SNOW, SATIN
AND SEDUCTION

Unwrapped by the Billionaire!

It's nearly Christmas and four billionaires are looking
for the perfect gift to unwrap—a virgin perhaps,
or a convenient wife?

One thing's for sure, when the snow is falling outside,
these billionaires will be keeping warm inside,
between their satin sheets.

**Collect all of these wonderful festive titles
in November from the Presents EXTRA line!**

The Millionaire's Christmas Wife #77
by HELEN BROOKS

The Christmas Love-Child #78
by JENNIE LUCAS

Royal Baby, Forbidden Marriage #79
by KATE HEWITT

Bedded at the
Billionaire's Convenience #80
by CATHY WILLIAMS

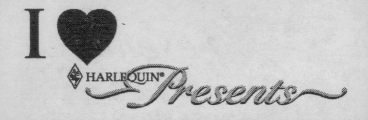

I ♥ HARLEQUIN Presents

BROUGHT TO YOU BY FANS OF HARLEQUIN PRESENTS.

We are its editors and authors and biggest fans—and we'd love to hear from YOU!

Subscribe today to our online blog at www.iheartpresents.com